Retro Spec

Retro Spec
Tales of Fantasy and Nostalgia

Edited by
Karen A. Romanko

Raven Electrick Ink

First edition, September 2010

ISBN: 978-0-9819643-1-7

Raven Electrick Ink
Los Angeles, California
http://ravenelectrick.com
comments@ravenelectrick.com

For Bob
and all the memories
we've yet to make

Contents

Introduction

Nostalgia, the dictionary tells us, is a bittersweet yearning for persons, situations, or things of the past. The past is a powerful lure, calling us back to relive events, some cherished, some reviled, some public, some private, and some affecting us to the present day. Our pasts are uniquely our own, yet we all share some elements, as though our lives were one-of-a-kind patchwork quilts, singular in pattern and form, but each containing some of the same patches as all the other quilts.

The shared patches on the quilts of our pasts are the province of *Retro Spec: Tales of Fantasy and Nostalgia. Retro Spec* uses the prisms of science fiction, fantasy, and horror to examine the culture, society, and politics of our recent past, the 1920s to the 1980s, in the United States and Europe. Twenty-six authors have contributed short stories, flash fiction, and poetry to the anthology, twining history with speculation to find out what happens when suffragettes construct robots, insects spread cultural movements, such as Art Deco, women carry out the first "manned" space flights, or hair metal bands make deals with the devil. Along the way, *Retro Spec* hits many of the major notches on the 20th century timeline, including World War II, the 60s counterculture, Chernobyl, and the fall of the Berlin wall, exploring and elucidating them by testing their limits with genre elements such as alien invasion, ghosts, alternate history, seers, and time travel.

Sometimes we'll cheer the wish fulfillment of these nostalgic speculations, sometimes we'll realize that history turned out better than we could have imagined, but, in the end, we'll understand the essence of each event or movement better than we did before.

Best of all, though, we'll remember.

Karen A. Romanko
Los Angeles, California
September 2010

Hula Hoop

Jude-Marie Green

The yellowed clipping did not disintegrate when Patty touched it. Raggedly scissored from the local paper, Sunday edition, September 1958. There she was, all sincere pigtails and straight bangs, Peter Pan collar on a white, swiss-dot, short-sleeved blouse and plaid knee socks that sagged to her ankles, exposing more than the usual collection of childhood scabs and cuts and bruises. Or was that her memory, imposing more on the photograph than the news camera could possibly capture?

The photo's caption said "Winner!" in letters now faded gray... showed her serious expression and her blank eyes which reflected the camera flash with two white—now yellow—glints in each pupil. She did not remember the photo being taken; she did not remember the end of that day; she remembered being afraid. Terrified.

Patty sat down hard on the attic floor, her jeans disturbing the dust and her legs in a strained tailor seat that had felt natural to her childhood legs but now stretched muscles uncomfortably and maybe a little immodestly. She could smell the clipping, even over the mustiness of the attic, the hint of mouse droppings and the ozone of the single electric light bulb hanging from the rafters. And the ghost of cigarette smoke over it all.

"Get me a pack of smokes," her mother had wheezed. She sat on the couch, her head down, coughing. No blood yet, that was years in the future, but the walls and ceiling were yellow from tar stains. "Keep the change, get yourself something."

A five-dollar bill. Patty, nine years old and fresh into the summer, wandered to that section of the liquor store that held all the toys, the bright plastic bottles of bubble soap, the balls, the games of jacks and pickup sticks, even comic books. *Weird Tales*, *Adventures on Other Worlds*, *Little Lulu*. Not a month ago Old Man Warner had put out a box filled with colored hoops, hula hoops. When she'd first spotted them, they'd called her name, sang it. She'd never even touched them. At $1.98, too pricey for her but not for the other kids. Now there were only two left: eye-searing yellow, blistering pink.

She could buy it. Her hand settled on the pink one: it spoke loudest. Did it sting her, a little electrical buzz? She held on tighter. She meant to try it right there but Old Man Warner growled from the counter where he slouched, watching her.

"You got money for that, kid?" He sounded doubtful.

Patty took the hoop to him. "This please, and a pack of menthols." She placed the five dollar bill on the counter top.

"For your mom, huh? Better not hear about you smoking," he said. He slid the money into his drawer and put a cellophane wrapped blue and white box down. "I'll keep the change against your mom's account," he said.

Mom looked asleep when she got home. Patty pushed the door shut and went to her room. She put the hula hoop under her bed; then she went back into the front room and put the cigarettes on the table next to her mom. She took the brown glass ashtray, overflowing with lipstick-stained butts and black and gray ashes, and emptied it in the kitchen trash can. She wiped out the ashtray and returned it to the table.

Her mom was awake now, working the cellophane off the pack. "Where's the matches?" she husked. She coughed and rapped the box against the table. She unwrapped the foil from the little square and shook loose a single white cylinder. "Well?"

Cold shock washed over Patty. She'd forgotten to take a book of matches from the fish bowl on the liquor store counter. A little sign taped to it said, "Free—to our customers!" She hadn't even glanced at the bowl, too entranced with her hula hoop.

She looked around, on the table, on the floor; and spotted a matchbook. She swooped it up and gave it to her mom.

"Forgot, huh?" The white tube hung from her mom's lips and seemed to suck in the flame all on its own. Her mom clicked her tongue. "Jeez. Where's the change?"

"Old...Mr. Warner kept the change. Against your account, he said." She did not back up when she said this. Retreat might cause Mom to chase her. She watched her mom's face. The lips tightened in a downward curve with the cigarette poking from the corner.

"Goddamned kid! I needed that money," and her hand flashed out and slapped against Patty's cheek, hard enough to sting. "Get out of here. Useless...." Mom continued to mumble around the cigarette but Patty fled.

She grabbed the hula hoop and opened the bedroom window and hoisted herself into the freedom of outside. Fresh summer awaited her and now she had her hula hoop.

She swung it over her head and gave it a twist to spin around her waist. She tried to bump it along with her hips but the loop just fell to the ground. She picked up her feet to step out of it; too new to crumple the plastic through carelessness! She picked it up and dropped it to her waist again. This time she kept it moving for a couple of seconds before the hoop fell again.

She worked with the hoop until her hair frizzled out of the pigtails and her face was flushed with effort and the sun had abandoned the sky, working towards nighttime. Sometimes when she spun the hoop around her waist, as she learned how to make the hoop travel from her knees to her armpits and back down again, but mostly circle her waist, sometimes she thought maybe she wasn't there in the yard. She was somewhere else, somewhere she had never been before; somewhere with sweet air and nice lawns and none of those things, just an absence of the ugly and worn-out that surrounded her. Yes, absence. She thought about that while her body learned to wiggle inside the hula hoop, while her muscles taught themselves how to keep the hoop spinning and her joints learned to bend and shimmy. She thought this might be a good place to stay, if she could get there. Better than her yard with the yellow crabgrass and dented trash cans and the brown oil stain under her mom's worn out car.

Her mom came out the door, wearing a shiny black waitress dress fitted to her curves, her hair teased into a brown bouffant. Fresh red lipstick shined around the cigarette that was always there.

"There you are! Time to come in; I have to go to work," she said.

She walked to the car door. "I left dinner for you in the oven. Make sure you're in bed before 9, okay?" She held out her arms. "Give me a hug."

Patty smelled Mom's makeup and perfume and hairspray and her mom's big black purse swatted her backside when they hugged. Mom kissed the top of her head. "Be good," she whispered. She got in the car and gave a tiny flip wave and drove off.

Patty sat on the front door stoop, a block of cold concrete, and listened to her hoop until the neighborhood was all dark. She pulled up her socks—they were always falling to rolls around her ankles—and stood. She liked the way the neighborhood smelled at night, and looked, all shadowy. She wouldn't be able to practice twisting the hoop inside. No way would she chance breaking something! But maybe she'd practiced enough for one day. She wanted to think about that place she went when she wasn't thinking. She smiled and went into the house.

It was 3 a.m. and her mom was screaming.

"Patty! Where the hell are my scissors? Patty!"

She rolled out of bed. Her mom didn't hit her, only threw the glass ashtray, which missed, in the few minutes it took her to find the scissors in the silverware drawer. Her mom snatched them from her hand and told her to go to bed, what was she doing up?

In bed, Patty pulled the scratchy Army blanket up over her head and hung on to her hula hoop.

The summer days belonged to her and she spent her time outside, practicing her hula hoop twirls and finding the doorways to that place. That place where nothing existed. Nothing bad, anyway. She never stayed long; she'd drop the hoop and the song would end and the glimpsed doorways would shut.

It was September and school was just about to start and her mom woke up long enough one morning to stop Patty before she ran out the door.

"You're really good with that hula hoop, huh?" her mom said. Patty stood with her hand on the doorknob. How would her mom know about that?

Her mom snickered. "My friends in the neighborhood tell me. Mrs. Tucker, Kenny's mother? She's especially interested. She gave me this." She held out a folded newspaper.

Patty stepped close enough to read the paper. A black-framed ad took up a quarter page and it blared HULA HOOPS! And CONTEST! And THIS WEEKEND! In much smaller print she saw the words "Entry fee." She relaxed away from the paper. No way could she afford anything.

"Well?" her mom demanded. "I think you'd be great. Might win something."

"What about the entry fee?" Patty said. "I don't have any money."

"No problem," her mom said. "Mrs. Tucker, she gave it to us. Said it was a healthy thing for a young girl." Mom's lips twisted into a cynical sneer. "Healthier than her son's habit of reading those nasty comic books!"

That's how Patty found herself dressed in her cleanest skirt and top, with new knee socks and polished saddle Oxfords on her feet, standing in the elementary school auditorium and twirling her pink hula hoop in front of everybody.

There was her mom, dressed up, skipping work to watch Patty compete. There was Mrs. Tucker, the benefactress, and her son Kenny, who wasn't watching her at all but reading a tattered comic book. There were other kids and other parents, strangers to Patty because she did not make friends. There was the newspaper reporter girl, taking notes with a pencil in a tiny notebook. There was the photographer, looking bored as he tried to find a comfortable position in the tiny wooden auditorium seat. There were the representatives from the toy company, the ones who'd sponsored the contest.

The representatives argued about giving her another hula hoop— new, not scarred and dented like her pink one. She shook her head and clutched her own hula hoop.

"Look, we have one in pink just like that one!"

She shook her head harder, almost crying; they could do things like take away her hoop, if they wanted, it was in the rules. She clung to her hoop and squinted her eyes closed against tears. No way would a fresh hoop have the same familiar magic as hers.

"Aw, let her keep it. This is all about fun, right, guys?" The representative waved her onto the stage with the other kids.

She stood under the spotlights and spun and twirled and wiggled, and the hoop circled her like a moon around her planet and after a while she found that nowhere place. She went away.

She wasn't gone for long. She came back when her hoop dropped and she hadn't won the contest but her mom kissed her anyway and her mom smelled different, not like cigarettes and horrid perfume but like talcum powder, and her dress was different, something like June Cleaver would wear and Patty didn't hurt anywhere and couldn't feel her bruises like big pits of ache and didn't itch to scratch out those scabs and her hair was longer and cleaner in the pigtails and they went out for an ice cream treat afterwards and her mom smiled a lot and they pulled into a long driveway at a nice home with green grass in the front yard and there weren't any yellow stains on the walls and she was happy, very happy, gloriously happy and she didn't use her hula hoop much and after a while forgot she had it and in 1972 when her mom died it wasn't from lung cancer and Patty's husband was at her side, holding her hand while her mom spoke her last words, I love you, to Patty, and Patty and her husband raised three children and sometimes in her dreams Patty remembered a time when she hurt a lot, something having to do with a hula hoop, and then one day Patty was old enough to die and she wondered if her life might have been different, she'd never had much pain or trouble in her life and those things were supposed to build character but here she was, happy, and she closed her eyes.

Someone smacked her shoulders, hard enough to move her feet forward, and someone else said, "And we have a winner, girl, it's okay, you can stop now, you won, girl!" And the first man smacked her shoulders again and her mom came up onto the stage and pinched her arm and said, "Don't make me look bad!"

Patty opened her eyes. She let the hula hoop drop. The toy company representative said, "All right folks! Let's hear it for this little girl who just hula hooped for five hours straight!" The relief in his voice grated on Patty's ears; why was he happy that she was back, was here? And where was "here"? Would her mom take her out for ice cream now?

Or hit her?

The photographer snapped her photo as she stood there with the hula hoop around her feet. She didn't smile for the camera; he didn't ask her to say cheese. He wanted to be out of there: nothing in the world as boring as watching kids all day long. She could hear his thoughts as loud as if he'd said them to her. The representative was thinking strange thoughts about her mom, something about being naked in bed; Mrs. Tucker was asleep and dreaming about eating a cat; her son, Kenny, was thinking he could be a superhero someday if only an alien race would give him a special ring. The other kids' thoughts came at her, clear and clean as alarm clock bells, and Patty put her hands to her ears to hold out their thoughts. She would not hear, she could not hear, she was deaf.

She screamed, then, and ran out of the auditorium. A jungle gym sat plumb in the middle of the yard and she climbed up it and stayed there, breathing hard. The dark sky above her sprinkled starlight down, but no moonlight. She looked for Sputnik but she'd never seen it before and did not see it now. She wouldn't cry, she wouldn't let herself cry.

Her mom stood at the foot of the jungle gym and stared up at her. "Patty, there you are. Come on down." Mom had a cigarette in her hand but she wasn't puffing on it. "Look, they gave me $25 because you won. Let's go get a treat, okay? At Helen Grace's? Hot fudge sundae?" Mom flicked ash from the tip of the cigarette.

The noise in Patty's head had dwindled to a bit of background static. She looked at her mom, who wore her shiny work dress, not the June Cleaver dress. Patty dropped down from the top rung and stood by her mom. The noise in her head faded.

"Ice cream," she said. "Thank you."

Her mom led her to the rusty old car. "You forgot your hula hoop," she chirped. "They said it was worn out; we could buy you a new one on the way home."

Patty didn't say anything but she wouldn't remind her mom about it. And her mom wouldn't remember on her own. They enjoyed the ice cream at Helen Grace, with the sugar pink smells and cold tile floors and red vinyl seats, and her mom talked a lot about school clothes and meeting new people, but she did not mention a new hula hoop again.

Patty never reminded her.

"Hey Mom! What ya doin' up here?"

"Putting things away, Tim," she said. She dropped the clipping back into the leather trunk, let down the lip, pressed her thumbs against the latch. It snicked closed.

Jude-Marie Green is the Associate Editor of *Abyss & Apex Magazine of Speculative Fiction*. She has had several short stories published, including "Hang Twenty" in *Sporty Spec: Games of the Fantastic.* Her collection *Glorious Madness* will debut in mid-2010. For updates see: http://judemariegreen.wikispaces.com

Invasion, 1955

Robert Borski

From seemingly out of nowhere they come,

not saucers, but their smaller ringworld brethren,

until almost everywhere you look

across the land, people are gyrating

in ecstasy, caught up in invasion frenzy.

Encircled, in fact, like the planet Saturn,

we twirl and twirl—unbeknownst to us,

further generating power in the piezo-

nanoverse of the invaders.

Soon, however, we're all as breathless as post-coital

lovers—yet who can keep this up forever?

No one. And so later, due to inertia or perhaps

boredom—the aliens never bother to teach us

the dizzy intricacies of their language—the castoff

hoops are relocated to the garage or attic.

Alternately, to avoid accusations of Vichy-like

collaboration, the invasion is demystified

by deeming it a fad, a reversion in the social

contract to childhood through the medium

of a shared ubiquitous toy.

Not that the aliens care for explanations

one way or another. Like brides abandoned

at the altar, they wait still for suitors that may

or may not ever come, hoping if not for outright

conquest, at least to betroth us.

Robert Borski's poetry appears regularly in *Strange Horizons* and *Star*Line*. His poem "Reel People: The Extra's Lament" was published in *Cinema Spec: Tales of Hollywood and Fantasy*. He lives in Stevens Point, Wisconsin.

Storm on Fifth Avenue

Neil Coghlan

By the summer of 1930, the new Empire State Building at Fifth Avenue and 34th Street was approaching sixty stories. Harry Holder, riveter, was earning thirteen dollars a day and anything he didn't spend in the speakeasy near the site or on tickets to go and see Babe Ruth bat for his beloved Yankees, he gave to Cathy his wife back home in Hell's Kitchen.

The last decade had finished with so much despair for Harry and millions of others like him: the Wall Street crash that he hadn't understood, rich bankers throwing themselves into the air from tall buildings, so much unemployment and strife. Here, though, was a city awakening from an economic slumber and raising itself to the sky.

That summer in the city was scorching. There were days that the sky boys, as those working on the metal skeleton were called, feared the very steel they walked on would start to buckle and bend in the heat, so intense was it.

Harry, working furiously with his rivet gun, would marvel at the speed the building was leaping bodily towards the clouds. There were quieter times, of course, when he would sit astride one of the massive girders and look over a smoggy city; the automobiles, the people, the few remaining horses, even the streetcars, would seem to Harry like the tiny plastic pieces of a game. He would stretch out his hand and hold it there, in mid-air, hovering over a vehicle or even a small building, feeling like a god.

One August morning, up on the east side of the 58th floor, the top floor as it then was, Harry was sitting by Paul Delvecchio, on a newly-hoisted girder that was lying on the cement floor.

"There are times up here that I get to thinking about all I've left behind, the family I'll never see again," said Paul suddenly.

"What do you mean?" Harry asked.

Without another word, Paul stood and walked out onto a girder, overlooking Fifth Avenue hundreds of feet below.

"I get so melancholy thinking about all of this."

Harry now stood too and walked to the girder where Paul was. It was second nature to these men working here to leap around the tower's steel bones, but something in Paul's demeanor unsettled him.

Paul looked back to Harry and smiled. It was a smile full of peace, a smile that spoke genuine warmth to a fellow worker who he'd known for eight months since they'd met on that chilled first day of construction.

"Tell everyone I'll miss them," he said. "Tell them I swam home."

And with that, he simply dropped over the edge. Harry fell into a horizontal position and looked over as his friend plummeted, finally falling out of sight.

Another incident the following day spooked the men further. Barney Schultz swore to them he'd seen the sea as he looked south.

"That is the sea, Barney! What did you think it was, the damn

Mississippi?"

Barney waited for the loud laughter to subside, then spoke with a glassy stare in his eyes.

"As God is my witness, I saw waves off the southern wall of this building. I saw the white crests of the waves, men. I watched the foam being blown off the top and whipped straight across in front of me."

The men gathered around Barney, eating their simple lunches, all stopped their chewing and listened.

"I closed my eyes twice and she was still there, the sea. New York was gone, men. From here to here," he said, raising his voice and sweeping his arms across him, "were the roughest waters you've ever seen. And I got to feeling mighty lonely, mighty sad. It was everything my own determination could do to stop me from getting out onto one of those girders and jumping."

On hearing this, Harry spoke.

"That's what Paul said yesterday before he jumped. Melancholy. That's the word he used."

Few of the cynical riveters believed in anything other than stress-induced hallucinations. Within a day or two, the industrial process that had seen the Empire State rise like a waking, stretching giant, surged the tower past sixty floors and the two odd incidents were forgotten.

The glaziers moved onto the 58th and 59th floors in the fall, as Harry and his fellow girdermen were working nearly thirty floors above.

One morning, in early October, John Cartwright was the first to arrive at the site. In the chilly gray light that came into the unfurnished floor from the newly installed windows on the 59th floor, he looked at his watch. Just after seven.

He exited the elevator and froze. In the center of the floor, in the expanse of bare cement that had yet to feel the comfort of carpet upon it, stood an odd looking character in a formal suit.

"Excuse me, Sir?" said John as politely as possible, not knowing if the man was management.

The man didn't flinch, showing no sign of even having heard John's voice. John approached him. Something struck John as unusual about the man's clothes and, without the aid of artificial lights, it was a few seconds before he realized it was a military uniform. The closer John got, the more he could see this was a navy uniform, but no navy colors that he'd ever seen.

John looked at the stranger's feet and felt his heart stop. The man's legs appeared to disappear into the very cement he was standing on, just by an inch or two. He shook his head, telling himself it was the early hour and the poor light that was fooling him. Perhaps the man was an amputee and that explained the curious illusion.

"*Wie geht es dir?*"

John's year in Europe at the end of the Great War had taught him enough to know the man had addressed him in German.

"Listen, I don't speak German, only English. What are you doing up here?"

For the first time, the stranger turned to face John. Or almost. He seemed to be looking just a few inches to his right and John was instinctively shuffling a little in that direction to meet his gaze.

"I like the English. After all of this is over, they will be our friends again. They are the only ones who are our equals in Europe."

John was again staring at the man's feet, assuring himself that they didn't really disappear into reinforced concrete. He saw that the man was again looking out towards Brooklyn, to the southeast, so looked there himself.

The great city of New York was waking to another day of opportunity. Along the East River, tugs buzzed around huge merchant vessels, passenger liners heading for Europe. Others pushed giant piles of timber. Along every horizon in every direction, a thousand factories spewed steam and smoke into the air. The machine, oiled by the good people of New York, was revving into action, even at this early hour. John turned to the military man to tell him how much he marveled at the big city from here up high—and he was gone.

In an instant, John had spun around, but the entire floor was empty. He got down on his knees and examined the spot where the man had been standing, the very point where his feet had seemed to disappear. There was nothing there.

By the end of the morning, the whole tower was ablaze with the tale of the navy ghost. Others recollected the summer events and it seemed that everything was centered around the 58th and 59th floors.

Under the threat of strike action, the builders, the Starrett Brothers, looked into any past worker deaths, but turned up nothing. Someone suggested investigating the materials themselves and that's when the curious case of the salvaged steel came to light. The site manager addressed the workers one lunchtime.

"We've made some investigations and it seems that the girders used up on the 58th and 59th floors were made using steel that was salvaged from a ship."

"What ship? The goddam Titanic?" shouted one of the men and the rest erupted into laughter.

"It was called the *Blücher*, a German battleship sunk in 1915 off England and salvaged a few years ago. I don't know what else to tell you."

"I think it's all a crazy coincidence myself," said one of the foremen. "We're thirty floors above there now, so we keep going, finish the damn building and let's cut out the ghost story baloney, OK?"

Everyone murmured their agreement.

By the spring of 1931, the Empire State had raced past the Chrysler Building and taken the title of world's tallest building. Harry Holder, Barney Schultz, John Cartwright and thousands of others finished their jobs and left to work on other sites, marry other women, father other children and live the rest of their lives far from the polished glass and marble of the magnificent tower they had helped put into the sky.

The stories of the construction site were passed on from man to man, generation to generation. Harry told his brothers the story of the man who jumped off the 58th floor to swim home. Barney entertained his children with tales of the day he'd seen the sea from a tower high above New York, and John Cartwright spoke with local historians about the sinking of the *Blücher*, then quietly laid it all aside and concentrated on his six children.

* * *

The smooth notes of "Three Times A Lady" wafted through the open plan office on the 58th floor. It was 3.52 a.m. and Wes King, chewing on a candy cigarette, wanted to go home.

By 1978, Wes's Company Clean was desperate to impress Pitman Publishers, a publishing company that had fired its way through five other cleaning companies in its twelve years of existence, thanks to the cleaners' outlandish claims of seeing things both inside and outside the building.

"Come on, girls. Let's finish up and get out of here," he shouted.

Carol and Lucinda were cleaning the boss's office. Wes approached the window and looked out. He couldn't see anything, so cupped his hands to block the office lights behind him. He realized he was looking out at what appeared to be a dark, tumultuous sea.

"Well, I'll be..."

His eyes caught a single light on the horizon, but the peaked wave caps took it from his sight every couple of seconds. As he stared out more intently, he became aware that the window was now fully under the water and he could hear the water slapping noisily against the top part of the glass. Feeling a tightening in his chest, Wes was having problems breathing.

He stepped away from the window, but suddenly there was a low knocking sound on the glass. Taking two steps back to the pane, he once again cupped his hands and found himself an inch from a face on the other side of the glass, bloated and decomposed, the lower lip almost fully torn away. The man was dressed in a simple sailor's uniform, his eyes open and staring upwards, upwards to the surface, upwards to the life and light that were gone forever.

Wes blinked and it was all gone. Again the lights of Manhattan were laid out below in a shining patchwork. Wes was trying to comprehend what had happened, his head pounding and sweaty, when he heard Lucinda screaming behind him.

"Put them out! I'm burning. Put them out, someone!"

Lucinda ran right past Wes, arms waving wildly, her eyes not even registering his presence, and crashed straight through the plate glass window. He watched in horror as she fell towards the streets. Raising his head to look at the hole in the window, he saw there a sliver of her flesh, caught on a jagged spike of glass, waving in the strong gusts that now blew in from the cold night. And the taste of salt on those stiff breezes was unmistakable.

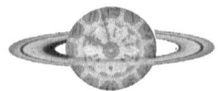

Neil Coghlan began writing fiction six short months ago. His work is slated for publication in *Bards & Sages Quarterly* in 2010. He is a 40-year-old Londoner presently living in Buenos Aires on a sabbatical year. He has taught English around the world for the last 15 years and is enjoying this new experience of writing. He also runs an educational website and scribas.com, a site dedicated to nostalgia.

Rain Goddess: The Dust Bowl, 1930s

K.M. Praschak

Malign winds claimed the earth,
scattering dust all the way to Chicago,
New York State, and the surprised sea.
Inside the prison of their barns, farmers wept.

In my enforced sleep, I heard curses from Texas
to Saskatchewan as the land began to fail.
Cotton, wheat, and other crops
yielded only pain to their overseers.

Some thought to escape west
to paradises of orange groves,
only to harvest more bitterness
as their children starved on low wages.

A new leader, elected by hope, sent forth
several tribes of relentless wizards
to fight for the remaining soil, to seek me out,
and to aid the horror-stained.

Other magicians toted cameras,

microphones, and stylus-shaped wands

all over the High Plains, trying to

capture Despair's thinnest shadows.

Sacrifices of pigs as well as

half-dead cattle brought money

back to many pockets; families

suspected their babies would live.

Over endless acres and dark seasons,

the diligent warriors worked together

to plant millions of young trees, and taught

reluctant farmers a different system of beliefs.

Just as the world's other conflicts caught you all,

my cloudy-eyed sisters and I escaped

our captors' Olympian traps, bringing storms

for your parched hearts, breaking the drought.

No longer lost, the red earth rests in winter.

Oklahoma writer **K.M. Praschak's** poems have appeared in *Star*Line*, *Abyss & Apex*, and *Sporty Spec: Games of the Fantastic*. Her science fiction novella "Paragon" is part of the *Amityville House of Pancakes 3* (Creative Guy Publishing). She serves as an acquisitions editor for the magazine *Tales of Moreauvia*. When she's not writing speculative poems and stories, she writes personal finance articles. The Dust Bowl's impact on North America and the tremendous response needed to overcome its effects still amaze her.

The Mustache

Lyn C. A. Gardner

In the early '70s, Aunt Julia and Uncle James toured the states by motorcycle. From coast to coast, they played in coffeehouses and bars as the folk duo James & Julia, earning just enough to keep going, sleeping under the stars. The picture on Mama's dresser showed a young woman with straight dark hair cut in bangs like Mama's, an upturned nose, and twinkling eyes. Colorful postcards arrived from all over the country, signed James & Julia in her looping hand. Mama complained that she sent cards to avoid sharing any real news.

In May 1974, I met Aunt Julia and Uncle James for the first time. Their motorcycle roared up our hill in a cloud of dirt. I'd never seen one in person, only Evel Knievel on TV. The helmeted figures reminded me of the astronauts whose round, reflective heads bobbed as their big-wheeled buggy rolled across the moon. Beside Aunt Julia, Uncle James was a giant. His brown hair curled over his collar, and he had the biggest, bushiest mustache I'd ever seen. Mama muttered, "It looks like he's got a rat attached to his lip."

Striding up the porch, Uncle James shouted hello and thrust out his hand. Aunt Julia laughed and crouched in front of the wicker chair where I hid, the fringes of her suede jacket swinging. Large blue flowers covered her cream pants; a beaded headband paralleled her bangs. "You must be Isabelle. I hope I have a little girl as beautiful as you!"

I crept out. "Do you want to swing?" The tree swing was off-limits without an adult. I led her by the hand. She lifted me onto the broad, flat seat and pushed me higher than Daddy did, telling me about the rolling hills of Kentucky, the flatlands of Kansas, the wildflowers of Colorado. Mama had to call us twice for dinner.

At the table, Mama was terse. I was too shy to talk in front of big, hairy Uncle James, who sat in my usual place beside Daddy, flashing his teeth in grins that parted the bushy mustache.

I slept at the foot of my parents' bed in a quilted sleeping bag while Aunt Julia and Uncle James used my room. In the darkness, Mama whispered, "He's going to get her killed!"

"You don't know that, Henrietta."

"Remember when Julia was in the hospital last year?"

"She had a miscarriage."

"He's so reckless she fell off the bike! She could have broken her neck!"

"It's her life."

"James has her hypnotized! She told me they don't *need* to get married. I don't want them staying here and corrupting Isabelle. Did you smell what he was smoking?"

Daddy sighed. "I've already spoken to him. He won't bring it in the house."

"I don't know why she stays with him. That hippie hair—that horrible mustache! They can't even afford a motel. Julia says they camp beside the road using saddlebags for pillows."

I exclaimed, "That sounds like fun!"

"Wisdom from the four-year-old," Mama said with disgust. The sheets rustled, the springs creaked, and they were silent—until Daddy began to snore. Across the hall, Uncle James answered in long, grumbling growls that rivaled Daddy's, who always said he was a father bear protecting his mate and cubs. I giggled as one snore paused and the other ripped to fill the silence in loud competition.

While my parents slept, I slipped down next morning to find Aunt Julia. Sitting on the porch with cigarettes and coffee, she told me about her adventures. I showed her my hiding place under the pines and the gravel lot by the college where the killdeer laid their eggs. We walked in the woods; she taught me plants and animal prints. She brought out her guitar and we sang along with my favorite records, The Carpenters and Peter, Paul and Mary, while Mama used Spic and Span on the kitchen floor and scrubbed my brother's diapers.

Uncle James scared me. He had to stoop through doors, and his booming laugh and flashing teeth sprang from behind that mammoth mustache like the fanged bear from the tree in my pop-up book. When I watched *Sigmund and the Sea Monsters*, he joked about the plot and mocked my favorite monster as a man in a floppy suit.

I ran outside to find Aunt Julia. She sat in the swing, drifting in slow circles, one toe on the ground. She stared at the lake through the trees with an expression that reminded me of Mama reading Aunt Julia's postcards.

"What's wrong, sweetie?"

"Uncle James is mean."

"Oh, honey, don't mind him. He likes to tease. He doesn't mean anything by it."

"I don't want anything bad to happen to you." I started to cry.

She lifted me into her lap. "Nothing's going to happen, sweetie," she murmured. Her thin arms held me, gentle but strong, as the ground fell away and slid back. "You're talking about the accidents, aren't you?"

"Yes," I said cautiously.

"It's not his fault, you know. No matter what your mother says." I heard iron in her voice. "When you're a performer, you've got to expect jealous fans and slashed tires. That fire was faulty wiring, and James got me out in time. And the night I hit my head, something big ran in front of the bike. James swears it was a bear." She laughed ruefully. "He's very protective of me. He's a big teddy bear himself."

This didn't sound like Uncle James, but I didn't know how to put my fears into words. "That mustache—"

She laughed. "You can't be scared of a mustache! It's only fur. I'm sure he'll let you touch it to see how soft it is."

"No!"

She took me inside and we crafted animals and birds from construction paper. Then she cut out a big black wave. Those twin handles with shaggy ends terrified me. "It's Uncle James's mustache," she said, laughing. "See? It's not scary."

When it got too close to my face, I burst into tears and ran away. Aunt Julia was still laughing as she called apologies.

Lying on the floor in my parents' room, I looked through the balcony's glass door. A lumbering shape crossed our yard. Big as a bear, it undulated like a worm, disappearing behind the garage.

Daddy's snores drowned out the sleeping bag's zipper and the musical floor. My bedroom door stood open. Asleep, Aunt Julia faced me. The rest of the bed was empty.

I climbed down the banister to avoid creaking stairs. Through the hall window, a ripple entered the woods where Daddy and I cut Christmas trees.

Outside, the chill night felt magical and frightening, like my favorite storybook, *Hildilid's Night*. I stepped off the weathered porch with the thrill I felt jumping into the lake.

The night wood looked scary; random limbs jutted from endless black. A howl rose, followed by snarls and crashes. Something dragged itself on all fours. Uncle James collapsed at my feet. "Get help, kid," he panted, his face streaked with blood—his upper lip bare.

It followed him. Its hairy back dipped in the middle. It had no eyes or face.

I screamed.

"Go inside, Isabelle!" Daddy shouted. Carrying a pointed shovel, he stood protectively over Uncle James. The beast swelled, puffing out its chest. It stretched sharp needles toward Daddy.

I ran in front. "Leave him alone!"

"Isabelle, stand back—"

The thing lifted its tentacles—

Roaring up the hill, a black bear hit the monster. Flashing claws and teeth—rolling fur—thunderous growls! Under the double-humped monster, thousands of brown legs waved red tips. The monster tore hunks from the bear's straight black fur. Despite her wounds, the bear flung herself at the monster whenever it neared Uncle James. Daddy thrust the shovel at its groping cords, cutting wiry hair. The monster dwindled, but the bear's blood smeared the grass. She panted—then spoke.

That voice! I'd fallen in love with that voice even before I heard its dark richness rival Karen Carpenter's. "Leave him alone or he'll shave you! Hurting him hurts you!"

The monster knocked the bear—Aunt Julia—into Uncle James. He groaned. The monster darted forward. Daddy plunged the shovel deep into its center.

Uncle James howled. Blood spurted from his upper lip. The bear swiped the shovel away to ring against a tree. I ran to fetch it.

The bear demanded, "Why are you hunting us? I thought you were another woman—another bear! But you're only his mustache! What do you care if he loves me?"

"I hate kissing you!" the mustache wailed. "He never thinks of me anymore! He never grooms me, just lets me grow wild! I was meant to be a handlebar, not a walrus! It's your hippie influence!" It curled like a spider and sobbed.

The bear's paw changed to a thin hand. She stroked the long fur of that faceless beast. "I don't like to criticize. I got too much of that from my mother. That's why I took to the road—"

"You dropped out because you became a bear," the mustache said cynically. "You couldn't handle it, an everyday girl from Queens. I

39

know the whole story. But the real question is, did he grow me to express himself—or has he changed to match my image?"

Uncle James croaked, "No one tells me what to do!"

Aunt Julia was so tired she morphed into a woman. Without her fur, I could see angry red scratches and welts, open wounds, a deep gash down one skinny, muscular leg. The mustache struck. Daddy hacked. Uncle James groaned. The mustache shrank, but wouldn't stop. What could I do? I was just a little girl who spent her days playing with paper, constructing houses from shoeboxes and cutting out pictures from catalogs to make storybooks.

I raced back to the house. Where was it? Aunt Julia had put the paper and scissors away before I returned for dinner. I dumped my writing desk drawer. Rooting, I found the stark, black cutout.

"Isabelle, what are you doing out of bed? Where's your father?" Mama demanded.

I snatched the mustache. "I'll get him!"

I ran. Clumps of monster littered the grass. It crouched like a cornered beast. Each time it sprang, Aunt Julia brought out her claws.

I planted the paper mustache on Uncle James. It stuck to his blood. He looked surprised. The new mustache moved when he wiggled his lip, though it was a trifle stiff.

He sat up, cradling Aunt Julia. "What do you have to complain about?" he asked the monster. "I let you do whatever you want! I haven't cut you for ages. You've got a wicked reputation—"

"What good does it do me?" the mustache moaned. "No more intoxicating blondes! No more one-night stands! No hours waxing and shaping me until I look my best! She doesn't even *like* me—she thinks I get in the way of kissing!"

Uncle James looked at Aunt Julia in surprise. "Is that true?"

She nodded.

"You want me to shave it off?"

"I never said that." She sounded exhausted. "But honestly, James, don't you think that might be a good idea?"

He touched his lip. That unconscious gesture expected a real mustache to be there. And so it was.

The monster shrieked. Hair burst in all directions—dry, split, lifeless. Inside was nothing but air.

Uncle James smoothed his new mustache. The shape Aunt Julia had created looked jaunty and neat. "Do you like it?"

Aunt Julia's voice was rich with humor. "Better than the last one."

Daddy draped his jacket over her. "I'll call the doctor." He turned and saw Mama. She frowned, hands on hips, watching Aunt and Uncle kissing. Daddy's jacket slipped off Aunt Julia's bare shoulders.

"Just what do you think you're doing, subjecting Isabelle to this display? This isn't Woodstock!"

"Henrietta, she saved our lives."

Mama fell silent, looking at all that hair and blood. Finally she said, "Well, I'm glad you took my advice and trimmed that mustache!"

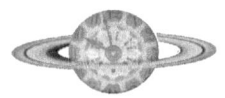

Catalog librarian by day, **Lyn C. A. Gardner** coedits the journal *Virginia Libraries*. She's had over two hundred poems, stories, and articles published in *Strange Horizons*, *The Doom of Camelot*, *Legends of the Pendragon*, *The Leading Edge*, *Horror Garage*, *Cinema Spec*, *Sporty Spec*, *Mythic Delirium*, *Abyss & Apex*, and more. Two stories and a poem earned honorable mention in *The Year's Best Fantasy and Horror* (12th, 13th, and 15th editions). Gardner is an associate member of SFWA and MWA and a graduate of the Clarion West Writers Workshop. Visit www.gardnercastle.com.

beat people

Bruce Boston

if beat people were the world
   man-high speakers
      would line the walls

there would be
   jazz for everyone
      cool and multiphonic

if beat people were the world
   there would be lots of poetry
      most of it very bad

berets and cheesy goatees
   and long existential novels
      would never go out of style

if beat people were the world
   coffeehouses and bookstores
      and cinemas would prosper

there would be

espresso in little china cups

and good smoke for everyone

the coolest sunglasses

would be from the goodwill

and all of our pads

would be a bit dirty

with mattresses on the floor

we dig it that way, man

if beat people were the world

it would always be night

with a cool-warm breeze

blowing wild

down the city streets

the perfect neon night

to groove on your senses

satori for everyone

and pass that jug of wine

Three-time Bram Stoker Award winner **Bruce Boston** is the

author of forty-five books and chapbooks, including the novels *The Guardener's Tale* and *Stained Glass Rain*. His work has appeared in *Asimov's SF Magazine*, *Amazing Stories*, *Weird Tales*, *Strange Horizons*, *Realms of Fantasy*, *Year's Best Fantasy and Horror*, and *The Nebula Awards Showcase*. In addition to the Stoker Award, Boston has received a Pushcart Prize, the Asimov's Readers Award, the Rhysling Award, and the Grand Master Award of the Science Fiction Poetry Association. For more information, visit his website at http://www.bruceboston.com/.

The Day Alan Turing Came Out

Leonard Richardson

Back in the 70s, computer magazines were full of programme listings, heavy on the numbers and uppercase letters. My fingers itch with muscle memory. LET this, PEEK here, POKE there. See a dog chase a cat, a submarine dodge depth charges. Or the one with all the patterns. Ooh, Turing's program, that beautiful one from the advert.

These days my fingers have it easier. They type into a search form:

model iv advert alan turing

The ICON accepts this without visible effort and produces a video image. In the video Alan Turing sits at a desk, hidden behind the static that veils anyone recorded from broadcast onto old analog tape.

Turing pretends the camera is not there. He has just covered a sheet of paper with formulae. He sets his pencil down and turns to the black and orange box on his desk. A keyboard and a computer, in one. He types genteelly, two-fingered, but rapidly. He types one final line of BASIC code.

The announcer makes his smooth, honed pitch. "There's doing maths," he says. Turing ignores him as well. "And then, there's *living* maths."

Turing reaches for the RUN button in the corner and my breath catches. This is the moment when I always found that I had mistyped a line and had to go through the magazine listing again, looking for errors. Turing does not worry. It's an advert. If he typed that last line wrong, they'll do another take. No reason not to be bold.

The screen moves. Cellular automata dance across the screen, slowly blossoming into the patterns on a peacock's tail feathers, rippling like the scales on a fish. All in black and white.

The camera zooms in on the unit itself and Turing disappears from the advert. "It's the new Model IV," says the announcer. "The first computer anyone can take home for under one hundred pounds. Another brilliant idea from Mycroft."

I leave the video running to see if there is a stinger, some amusing shot of Turing in his role as the nation's absent-minded uncle. There is none: Turing has left the set to collect his cheque. The video ends. My fingers move again:

turing cellular automata basic listing

"Alan Turing was gay, you know," says B.

"Aya?" B. has been looking over my shoulder while I drink deep the spring of nostalgia. Even my casual ICON browsing is not safe.

"Oh, yes. Gay as a...well, the usual similes don't apply, do they? Gay as a field mouse who happens to be extremely gay." B. rattles the ice in his glass, right next to my ear.

"Do you know this, or is it speculation? He's pushing computers on kids in 1980. They'd never hire a gay man for that."

"'s absolute fact. He came out a few years before he died. There was a pride march in Manchester in the late eighties. The first really big one, I think. And who's that shuffling down the middle of the street with the crowd but Alan Bloody Turing. They must have thought he was lost.

"He never said more than ten words about it afterwards, but yeah. Look it up. Absolute fact."

alan turing manchester pride march

The ICON sends me a still photo, and there he is. His beard now shaved, hands folded on a cane, wearing a three-piece suit and a medal instead of a friendly computer-selling jumper. This time he sees the camera, and is looking into it.

An open secret, as such things often were back then, between academics. Safe enough, but unsatisfying. And then one day—what is he afraid of, retired, a war hero, what can they do to him? One day Turing leaves his house in Manchester and walks up a street he walks all the time. And because of who he walks with on that day, communicates a datum.

His fellow marchers in T-shirts, looking at him or at the photographer. Wondering if his fame might combine with their numbers to offer protection from whatever happens next. Surprised by his archaic dress, as if he were posing for an old-fashioned portrait, not realising that photographs these days are developed in color.

Editor's note: The real Alan Turing, often called the father of modern computing, was prosecuted for homosexual acts, then a crime in Great Britain, in 1952. He accepted chemical castration in lieu of a prison term, and died in 1954, a probable suicide. In

2009, Prime Minister Gordon Brown issued a posthumous apology to Turing on behalf of the British government.

Leonard Richardson is an author of science fiction and technical nonfiction. His fiction has appeared in *Futurismic* and *Strange Horizons*.

These United States of Frankenstein: Meltdown

Brian Rosenberger

He was haunted by the word

No heed paid to his warnings

and who knew better the dangers

of science gone astray

Three Mile Island, a forgotten fairy tale

A trip halfway around the globe

to see containment-suited ghosts,

stacked bodies

enough to build a fortress

but still no protection

from the radiation

Mr. President breathed deep

calming the monster within

A man made of others' limbs—

the tears for Chernobyl's dead

are his and the world's

Brian Rosenberger resides in Marietta, GA. His recent and forthcoming credits include the anthologies *The Book of Tentacles*, *Side Show 2*, and *The Terror of Miskatonic Falls*, the magazines *Ghostlight* and *Hungur*, and several online publications. He is the author of the poetry chapbook *Poems That Go Splat*, and a new collection of his writing, *And For My Next Trick*, published by BeWrite Books, will be released in 2010. Additional updates can be found at http://home.earthlink.net/~brosenberger.

New and Improved

Jennifer Rachel Baumer

She almost didn't answer the door when he rang the bell. Martha Simon wouldn't say she was addicted to her shows, but she did hate to miss what was going on. With Bill at work all day and the boys at school until he picked them up after football practice, basketball practice or baseball practice, she had nothing else to do except pick up their socks and dishes and magazines and Bill's disgusting cigar butts. She'd have loved to have a girl, someone soft and pretty and quiet to spend afternoons with.

Though if Martha was going to be honest with herself, and she might as well since no one else ever listened to her, quiet afternoons with anyone was the last thing she wanted. She had enough quiet. Half of her friends were on those fancy tricyclic mood elevators because of the amount of silence in their lives between the departure and return of family and the amount of mind-numbing work done in that silence. And then on the weekends between televised sports and the boys' sports, she had enough noise. She thought she'd like to try something in between.

Or something altogether different.

Like those people in her shows, who were all married like Martha was but obviously it meant something else to them in Port Charles and Springfield, because they all had affairs and if they had children, those children weren't just seen and not heard, they weren't seen, either.

A commercial for laundry detergent came on and the man on the doorstep rang the bell again. Martha supposed he'd seen her through the window on his way up the walk, seen her sitting in her husband's easy chair and staring at the set. Still, she answered the door with her broom in hand as if he were interrupting her cleaning and she really needed to get back to it.

"Good afternoon, madam," he said, the first words out of any traveling salesman's mouth, unless they were "New and improved," and she was already planning her response, *No, thank you, the Ford is only two years old, a 1955, thank you, and we have all the insurance, oil, windshields, tires we need* or *My vacuum works just fine, thank you,* or, *I really don't need any more encyclopedias.*

She didn't, really. Martha was a sucker for encyclopedias and had to hide the last three sets from Bill and make up stories about what she'd spent the money on. It was just that the salesmen always talked to her about things in the books and asked her questions and made her feel so smart. They listened to her opinions and laughed at her jokes and the fliers were always brightly colored and glossy even if the resulting encyclopedias looked as if they'd been printed on newsprint with old ribbons.

The man standing on the steps in his shiny suit had been there long enough he now started to say, "Good afternoon, madam," again when Martha realized she was staring, her mouth gaping open.

She closed her mouth. Across the street Mrs. Turkelson twitched her curtains. *Get an eyeful, you old cow,* Martha thought, but Mrs. T was on tricyclics and wouldn't remember anything she'd seen five minutes from now.

I really need to get some of those pills, Martha thought and turned her attention back to the man on her porch. "What do you need?" she asked, and rattled her broom at him. *I'm busy. Can't you see I'm busy? Busy, busy, busy.*

Behind her in the living room, the show came back on. She had to force herself not to glance back over her shoulder. *That*, that was life, what was on those shows. What Martha had was a test pattern.

The salesman took a look over his shoulder, then glanced next door where Tilly Caulkins was ostentatiously shaking out a rug. He turned back to her. "Good afternoon, madam," he said for a third time. "I'm glad to catch you at home on such a beautiful afternoon."

Martha blinked. The day was scorching, early fall Southern California smoggy, but whatever. She didn't suppose honesty served door-to-door salesmen well.

In the next instant, he proved her wrong. "I need your *help*," he hissed wildly.

Martha opened her mouth to ask just what the dickens this complete stranger was talking about, and he shouted, "Get down!" He launched himself at her and drove her back through the open door onto the living room floor.

Martha struggled up from under him just as her front steps vanished in a blinding flash. The house shook. Martha screamed and buried her head.

"What the hell are you selling?"

It was the first thing that occurred to her. Whatever it was, she didn't want any.

"You're very important," he said, without explanation, and, "Where's your bathroom?"

Bathroom? Was he selling cleaning products? What the hell had happened to her front steps?

"*Bathroom!*" he shouted at her. "Focus, Mattie!"

Mattie? "Down the hall."

He half-dragged, half-pushed, shoved her into the tub as Martha heard footsteps coming toward them. She had time to see something enter the bathroom, something tall and human-shaped but with a long, twisted face like a mosquito and bulging eyes. Then the salesman turned on the water and flashed something in her eyes and Martha blinked hard —Mattie blinked hard—and she was somewhere else.

"OMG," Mattie said. "That body. Those boys. That house. Those dishes. The sheets, the dog—"

"Please," Jinx said from the controls of the time rider. "Just watching is enough."

"But I mean, I was going to. I mean, she was going to." She stopped, again, confused, and looked around the lab. Sparkling, bright, effortlessly clean, it pulsed with readouts from times spread across the boards. Almost too fast for her enhanced eyes to see, the screens lit with attacks taking place across the decades throughout the 20th century, from the flappers to the punks. Anywhere the insectile aliens thought they could get a toehold, Control had sent agents, sliding into acid-drenched hippies, ecstacy-ridden new-agers, tranquilized housewives, drunk flappers and dandies. Jinx had already turned away, bringing up 6972 Morning Glory Court where even now a team had erected deflectors and was scrubbing down the area where the stairs had been and pouring new concrete and all the while the thing blundered through the house, that cute little ranch house she had shared with Bill and the boys, and Martha felt a surge of indignation that something would come in to her home and—

"You all the way back yet?" Jon asked. He'd let the shiny salesman's suit fall away. He wore the same gleaming leather body armor Mattie did.

She ran her hands over her biceps and delts, made fists and reached for the weapons array that had just slid out of the war chest cabinet. "I'm awakened. Send me back. There are *bugs* in my *house*."

Jinx gave her a long look for that and Mattie winked. Jinx sighed.

"Jon? Going along for the ride?"

"Wouldn't miss it." He'd already shouldered two flamethrowers and a laser rifle. What did Jinx think he was going to do? Blow up Control?

The world shimmered and turned inside out and Mattie had a moment to wonder what Martha thought was going on, but poor anesthetized Martha with her dreams of drugs and reality of soap operas— she wouldn't remember a thing. And that seemed sad.

If she cleaned up enough this slide, she might not have to go back in that *body* again. Mattie shuddered and the shimmer cleared and she was dumped back into Martha's living room, body armor, weapons and all.

The bugs were pouring in. Jon shouted something she didn't get and they moved back to back, weapons whining as they fired up. Damned bugs kept coming and wouldn't Martha have a fit if she saw this? But maybe, Mattie thought, something about Martha just might enjoy cleaning house this way.

She pulled the trigger and a wall of flame danced out in front of her. The creatures fell back, flesh bubbling, eyes bursting. They screamed, always that mind-numbing, ripping scream that didn't sound like anything anyone could ever describe. Like death made sound. Then they charged, the flaming among them providing cover for the others, who trampled the bodies of their own to reach clawed legs at Jon and Mattie, and the two of them shouted, unleashed lasers and cutting weapons.

Jon yelled, "I'm hit!" but didn't fall.

The room hadn't caught fire. This one was lucky. The creatures fell under the assault. Martha's tattered-rag throw rug scorched and smoldered with bug juice. She'd wonder what had happened to it but things happened around Martha she couldn't explain. She lost time sometimes. Sometimes she had a desire for Something Else. Something different.

Something exciting.

Mattie realized she was grinning. "Martha might like this," she shouted at Jon. "I think she wanted *more*."

"They all did, sweet cakes," Jon said.

"Bite me, buttercup," she said, and "A girl likes a little fun in her days."

"I guess so."

But his voice sounded limp and as he gunned down the last of the bugs, Mattie turned her attention to the medkit, slapped a suture over the bug gash decorating his arm and did a quick X-ray for infection or poison before she turned back to the insects.

"Jinx?"

Jinx's voice held the usual time distortion through the com. "Area's clear. Looks like you two were right on top of the infestation. Good job. I can pull you out or—well, why not?"

Even as she spoke the rolled rug stuffed with burnt bug bodies shimmered and vanished.

The living room smelled funny but Mattie thought if she opened the windows it would clear out before nightfall.

Before Boring Bill and the Belligerent Boys got home.

The fire hadn't spread. The response team had finished with the stairs. She *could* go and just the thought of being dumped into that fat, slow, doughy body again—

"Leave me here a couple days, can you, Jinx?" she asked and Jinx's voice laughed through the years.

"Always the martyr."

Martha woke mid-afternoon, mouth dry and neck aching from the odd angle her head had tilted. "Oh, my goodness." The TV had turned to cartoons while she'd slumbered half the day away, her floors unswept, her dinner unmade and—she'd missed her shows.

She sat for a minute, sad about that. Bill always said nothing happened on those shows from one week to the next that any idiot couldn't figure out without watching, but she liked them. They gave her a little bit of something different.

A glance at the clock showed her it was almost four and she stood up, intending to get something to eat and start dinner and turn to her chores. But outside the day was beautiful, the heat of midday calmed to afternoon golden, and a small child ran by and Martha thought abruptly, *I want to do that* and went down the hall to the bedroom she shared with Bill. After a long time she found a pair of cotton shorts with an elastic waist, which still fit, and a big t-shirt of Bill's she didn't think he'd miss. She had a pair of Converse shoes she'd gotten for tennis when she'd played briefly in college. She took her hair down from its chignon and put it up the way she hadn't since grade school—in a ponytail.

"What are you doing, Martha?" she asked herself when she took in her own weird reflection in the mirror.

"Something different," the Martha in the mirror grinned back, and Martha went outside.

She didn't even notice when Mattie slid out of her and went back to her own time. She'd set her sights on the rose bushes halfway down the street, ignored the niggling feeling that she ought to go spray the roses for *bugs* and get on with dinner, and then, rose bushes firmly in sight, the new and improved Martha ran.

Jennifer Rachel Baumer lives, writes and runs in Northern Nevada, where she shares her life with her husband, Rick, and more felines than makes sense, both reformed ferals and unreformed domestics. Her work has been published in genre magazines and anthologies, including *On Spec* and *Lady Churchill's Rosebud Wristlet*, and she makes her living writing articles about everything from the economy to art.

Sparks between Our Teeth

Amanda C. Davis

I smoked a lot
In the Fifties.
Half a pack a day.
Helped with my nerves
When the job needed done.
We were shrewd and urbane,
Chronos cowboys,
And pretended we belonged to the era
And didn't know better.

Killing spies and profiteers.
Keeping kinks out of the timeline.
Vintage smoke made it all go down easier.

I quit when they transferred me
To the twenty-first century.
It's not the same, anyway,
Crushing butts beside your computer
Instead of in a nightclub
In a suit.

But sometimes on the sidewalk

I pass a man

Puffing something sweet and stinging

As my Chesterfields used to be,

And it all comes back:

Gin and Reds and social shaming,

High heels and discretion,

Careless racism,

Constant fear.

Choosing cigarettes

On your doctor's recommendation.

Tracking a timesquatter to his portal,

Fixing his mistakes,

Unsnarling his damage,

Throwing his body

Where the G-Men can't go.

And a smoke under a street light

To put you back together.

We choked our lungs with tar

Just like everyone around us,

But cold foreknowledge

Set us apart from the natives:

We knew about carcinogens.

We were trying to kill ourselves.

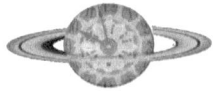

Amanda C. Davis is a Pennsylvania engineer with a green thumb, a growing collection of comic books, and a fondness for pulpy horror. Her work has appeared in *The Town Drunk*, *Dog Oil Press*, and *The Middle of Nowhere: Horror in Rural America*, among others. Visit her at http://www.amandacdavis.com.

Chalk Circles

K. Curran Mayer

Griffin paused in the door of the Scrying Room. The mirror-covered walls gave an impression of a crowd of women. But in the center of them stood the one real person—his wife, staring thoughtfully at the chalked circles on the floor.

Then she looked up and saw him. Her concentration sharpened to a razor intensity. "Stop there." She would have seemed angry to a stranger. Dozens of reflected eyes bored into him. He didn't mind that as much as he minded the ones who stared off into the depths of the mirrors. He always wondered what those eyes saw.

Griffin sighed. "Don't worry. I'm not coming in." Even when he was a student himself—a promising student, back then—he'd been banned from the Scrying Room. He was too good at seeing things.

"I brought you these." He lifted his hand to show her the bouquet of roses. His thousand reflections lifted a garden's worth of floral tributes. "How were the Games today?"

Amelia only bared her teeth in a too-rigid smile and shrugged. "Jesse Owens won another medal." She turned her attention back to the chalked circles of protection on the floor.

Griffin followed her gaze, then glanced at the battered little Focusing Table by the door. Today the table had only a shallow dish, where an enchanted flame burned without heat or apparent fuel. Griffin remembered her mentioning that it had been a student's idea. That

Applegate boy had thought a symbol of the Olympic flame would help hone in on the Games, and Amelia had to admit he was right.

"When will you be done?" Griffin asked, though he knew full well that she could stay on indefinitely, triple-checking and quadruple-checking all the elements of the spell and the Safety circles. Tomorrow was the big event, when the magical duelists competed. A few of the faculty probably would decide to wander into the elective scrying workshop for that. Griffin was the only person who knew that Amelia cared what they thought of her, as the first female professor in their ranks.

Amelia shrugged again. Then she got to the point. "We almost lost one today."

Griffin lowered his hand, half-hiding the flowers behind his trouser-leg. He wished he could hide the scent of the flowers, too. "Who was it?" he asked, though he knew that answer, too. *"Haven't had such a — sensitive student since you and your brothers, Griff,"* Professor Nickel had said, when Roland Applegate entered Wyland College's gates two years before.

"That Applegate," Amelia said on cue. "Young idiot stepped outside of the Time-Safety Circle. Went wandering off somewhere—the past, I think. It must have been the past."

Griffin heard the quiver in her voice. He took a step into the room, despite Amelia's hiss of warning. He knew better than to put a toe over the first chalked line. He just put the flowers down on the table beside the little lamp, and held out his arms.

She came and hid her face on his chest. It reminded Griffin of how she had clung to him that one time years ago in Gallipoli, with her nurse's cap askew.

He sighed, feeling more helpless than usual. He could predict what people would say before they said it, but he never seemed to know how to comfort the woman he loved. "Come home and have some tea," Griffin suggested eventually. "You know you'll be here early tomorrow."

As Amelia locked the door behind them, Griffin thought he saw a flicker of movement down the passage. But when he turned, it was gone. He hesitated over mentioning it, then decided against it. No need to worry Amelia now if he was starting to see things again.

Amelia slipped an arm through his as they turned out of the college gate. "Sometimes I wonder why we bother." She glanced both ways before crossing the street, though in the Long Vacation the traffic was always gentler than in term-time. "All those students stayed up during the vac. for this, and yet, these days there's the television—"

"Scrying is more—intense, I suppose," Griffin said wryly. He tucked her arm more firmly through his. He could feel the rough tweed of his coat prickling through his shirt at the pressure.

"That isn't worth losing a mind." Amelia let out a breath. "But the silly cuckoo was just fine, so it's all right."

"Yes." For a minute, Griffin resented the words. *All right.* Of course things were all right, on some level. But sometimes as he sat across from Amelia at the breakfast table, reading the headlines of murder and Madrid upside down, he felt as if they were all playing a great game of All Right.

"And it was lovely of you to bring—" Amelia broke off. They

stopped walking simultaneously, as they realized that the roses were still back on the table.

Amelia didn't need to explain flowers to the senior faculty in the morning. Griffin turned. "I'll run back and get them. No, trust me, I know where it's safe to step."

He knew she was tired when she actually did hand him the iron key to the Scrying Room. Griffin was always startled by the weight of the iron keys that locked all the most dangerous rooms of the college. As a mere secretary in the college, he never had call to handle such keys, and he always expected the lightness of more easily-enchanted metals.

He leaned down to brush a kiss on her cheek. "Go ahead and put the kettle on."

As Griffin reached the door of the Scrying Room, he paused. Was it his imagination, or was it slightly ajar? He turned the key over and over in his pocket. Now the weight of the iron was reassuring.

As he touched the door with his fingertips, it swung slowly inwards.

Young Applegate stood in the center of the room, with his eyes rolled back in his head so that they gleamed as white as cataracts. A galaxy of matching white eyes stared through Griffin from every side of the room.

Griffin's fingers twitched on the key again. If Amelia were here, she would know what to do, she would snap into efficiency and seize control of the mirrors somehow. She'd always had a knack for knowing what was safe to see and forcing the mirrors to show only that.

He edged forward, then looked down to check where the circles were.

Only the outermost circle remained. It was a few inches from his shoes. But beyond that—the floor by Applegate's feet showed only smudged outlines.

As Griffin watched, Applegate began to spin in a slow circle. The reflections spun with him, one dizzy curve after another.

Griffin remembered that—how could he ever forget that desperate search for a way out? By now the boy had realized that he was almost out of time, that soon he would forget that everything he saw around him was just a skewed reflection. A professor's hand on his arm had dragged Griffin back from that edge, all of those years ago.

There was no time to get a professor. Griffin stepped forward over the last protective circle.

Gunfire. He could taste the acridness of burnt gunpowder in the air. No gas yet, though, praise heaven. He had no gas mask. Griffin looked back over his shoulder. The little flame by the door was lost in a horizon red with distant fires. Was the door still back that way?

He should have gone for help. Even when he was the brilliant young scholar, he hadn't been able to cope with the Scrying Room. And now he was the shellshocked secretary that old Nickel kept on for pity. So instead of just the boy, there would be two souls lost.

Someone shouted to duck, and Griffin threw himself down in the mud before he realized that the cry had been in German. He had learned the language during his studies long before he ever carried a gun—

He waited for shelling to start, but there was only silence. Around him, other uniformed men kept moving steadily through the shadows with packs on their backs. Griffin dragged himself cautiously back up to his hands and knees.

He had been looking for something. His mask, where was his mask? No—something else—the boy. Where was the boy?

There. The one who wasn't moving. Griffin stumbled up and slogged through the mud to the boy's side. Young Applegate's eyes were still turned up white, the way they had been in the Scrying Room, as if he was about to faint. He was in a uniform, too, not quite like the uniform that Griffin had worn for so long that it seemed like a second skin.

He reached out and seized Applegate's arm, then lurched back, turning, turning, trying to find the door.

Was that a distant smell of roses? Griffin swung his head from side to side, trying to hone in on the smell. The harsh gunpowder-smoke seemed to scrape the inside of his nostrils as he inhaled over and over again. Please heaven, he begged silently, just preserve us from the gas a little longer. Just a little longer—

He closed his eyes, shutting out the murk and the uniforms. Amelia would be making the tea now, and he had flowers to bring her. He walked blind, still dragging the boy with him. He heard another shout behind him, and broke into a jog—

He crashed into the door, then felt the impact of Applegate beside him. Griffin hardly felt the pain in his shoulder. He just leaned against the slick mirrored surface, gasping on the smells of chalk and roses.

For a moment he didn't dare look over his shoulder at the

mirrors. What if he saw himself and young Applegate reflected in uniform, surrounded by a platoon's worth of reflections?

When he finally ventured to turn, he reached for the bouquet. In the room beyond, a thousand Griffins did the same, each of them clad in his old tweed coat. Amelia had left a chalky hand-print on his sleeve, he noticed. Then he averted his eyes, still afraid he would spot a reflection somewhere among his thousand selves that still wore the uniform like a wrinkled skin.

He looked instead to the boy beside him. The boy's gaze was more normal now, a fawn-eyed brown; but Griffin noted that the pupils were dilated with shock.

"Let's get you to the infirmary, Applegate," Griffin said, his voice as hoarse as if he had just been breathing real smoke instead of reflections.

Applegate nodded. The boy had recognized his spoken name, at any rate.

As they exited the Scrying Room, Griffin locked the door firmly behind them once again.

"I picked it," the boy said suddenly, as if he had known that Griffin was about to ask how he had got in. "With a spell. I won't get sent down, will I?"

Griffin sighed. "I don't know," he said. He thought, *Amelia will have made the tea now. It will be bitter by the time I get back to her.*

He passed a hand over his eyes. He meant to sound angry as he demanded, "Why on earth did you rub out the circles? Wasn't once enough, without trying it without the Safeties?" Even to his own ears, his voice was merely exhausted.

The boy stared down at his feet. "I couldn't keep it in the present, because I was trying to see tomorrow's Games," he mumbled. He added something indistinct about a bet.

Griffin bit his tongue on further questions. Something must have been important to the boy, to send him back into the room alone. Perhaps money, perhaps debt, perhaps honor. The Dean and Amelia could find out tomorrow.

For now, what was important to Griffin was to get home.

This is **K. Curran Mayer's** second published story set in the speculative world of Wyland College. The first one, in which Amelia appeared as a graduate student, was printed in Whortleberry Press's *Strange Mysteries* anthology in early 2009. Mayer's other short fiction credits that year included *On the Premises*, *Silver Blade*, and Lame Goat Press's *Horror through the Ages* anthology. When not writing, she spends her time on history, folklore, organic farmwork, and whatever day jobs she can find.

R101 Is Burning

Cliff Winnig

I kicked open the door just as the engine noise peaked. The *R101* would soon be underway.

Dr. Erich von Drachen sat up on his bed, mindful of the top bunk. He smiled boyishly—the airship's secret passenger, barred from public appearance.

"You might have knocked, *Fräulein*."

I smiled back. "Had you checked, you'd have found your cabin locked. Your friends do not entirely trust you, it seems."

He raised an eyebrow at that. "Interesting, Miss...?"

I entered swiftly. The damaged door did its best to close behind me.

"Keating. But please, call me Miranda."

He nodded and rose. A man in his mid-forties, he stood a bit taller than me, his amiable features framed by greying hair and a close-cropped beard.

"Ah yes. I saw your name on the passenger manifest. Lord Thomson's secretary, I believe. Thank you for visiting me. I'd been wondering who the MI5 agent would turn out to be." He picked up his jacket and began putting it on. He already knew we'd be going for a walk.

"What gave me away? The smashed door?"

"The gun, actually. I'm more used to smashed doors than you

might think. The Fatherland's politics have grown dangerous of late. I make frequent trips to England. Some at home do not like this."

I nodded. "I'm well aware." Three weeks prior I'd watched the National Socialists take nearly a fifth of the Reichstag seats. MI5 had concerns.

While every government has spies, since the War we paid special attention to German ones. When von Drachen suddenly vanished from his English laboratory, we'd traced him here. Him and his rather large pet robot, a prototype only he understood. The notes for all his inventions always lacked crucial details. We'd checked.

I waved my Webley at the abused cabin door. "Shall we?"

"I won't help you find it. Despite my international interests in the corporate sector, I will not have your government use it against Germany."

"May I remind you that I'm the one holding the gun?"

He nodded, his expression serious at last. "Of course. But you still can't make it do what you want."

"Trust me, *Herr Doktor.* I'm good at persuading the uncooperative." At .455 caliber, the Webley Mk VI is very good at persuading. When its considerable charms fail me, well, I've always admired its stopping power.

I stepped back, letting him walk ahead of me. We left the cabin and headed down the corridor. The rest of the passengers sat in the lounge or promenade, busy watching the *R101's* departure.

"I hope you are swift as well as strong, Miranda. I can assure you that revolver won't help with Fritz."

"Cute name for it."

"*Danke.* I named him after my late, lamented tabby."

Where the corridor turned left I slid aside a secret panel. Behind it lay the dim vastness of the superstructure. "My condolences. Through here, *Herr Doktor.*" Once inside, I'd make him lead.

The ship lurched as they released her from the mooring mast. We were underway. A second later the deck tilted alarmingly towards the nose of the ship.

The good doctor had been waiting for just that moment.

He slid a small flanged gun out of his sleeve and fired it at my feet. A crimson beam shot out, fusing the soles of my suede shoes with the deck. I cursed in a most unladylike fashion. They'd been from my favorite Paris boutique, and rather dear.

Von Drachen dove through the door, vanishing from sight.

I steadied myself on the wall as I slipped out of the ruined shoes. Time to ditch the rest of my street clothes. I followed him through the door, closing it behind me. He'd already disappeared.

I quickly stripped to my leotard and tights. I pulled a small backpack out of my purse and strapped it on. Ballet shoes, modified to grip any surface, completed my new ensemble.

I crept forward, mindful of a running crewman who'd no doubt been sent to release forward ballast.

After the initial shock, I'd grown used to the slanted decks, so I started after the doctor, threading my way to the bow. I moved carefully, not wanting any more surprises.

I heard the ballast being released, felt the ship level off.

This shouldn't take long, I thought to myself. I knew where to find the robot. Its weight had pulled down the nose of the ship, after all.

Seven hours later, I'd just about given up. I'd crossed every deck, eluding the busy crewmen sent to observe the effects of an ever-worsening storm. Thunder echoed through the superstructure at increasingly frequent intervals.

The robot, I'd decided, must be hidden in one of the bags of hydrogen gas. I'd made tiny incisions in a handful of likely candidates, but had seen nothing untoward through the holes. Crew movements had kept me from conducting a systematic search, and I feared I'd reach India with nothing to show for my efforts. The doctor would have some manner of in-flight escape, I was sure of it.

Another crash of thunder rolled along the ship. I calculated we must be over France. If he were still aboard, he'd be leaving the airship soon. Perhaps he'd only been waiting for the weather to clear.

Thunder came again, but this time I caught a hint of another sound: fabric tearing. Ducking behind a distracted crewman, I padded towards the source.

Nothing but gasbags, whole and undamaged.

Time to risk detection. I'd give the cover story to Lord Thomson and the captain, should it come to that. But I'd have little time to move once the crew spotted me.

I pulled out my torch from the backpack and shone it at the nearest gasbag. It looked empty of all but flammable gas.

The same with the next.

The third revealed an odd silhouette. Even allowing for the angle of the light, the robot had to be huge. I also saw that one seam appeared to have been undone and resealed from within.

"Hey!" yelled a voice behind me. "You there!"

No time left. I pulled out my knife and slit open the bag. The sealing agent proved tougher than the fabric, so I tore a jagged line of my own, parallel to the seam.

"Don't do that! You'll let out the gas!" I heard running footsteps approaching from two directions.

"*Alarm!*" The muffled voice came from within the bag. "Fritz— *schnell!*"

Switching the knife into my left hand, I cut a longer slit in the bag and prepared to leap inside. The Webley settled comfortably into my right hand. I'd have to be careful where I fired it.

Then came something I didn't expect, a bullet ricocheting by my head. At first I thought von Drachen had fired from within the gasbag, but then I knew: his accomplice among the crew.

I ducked and rolled, coming up in a *grande plié* with the gun in both hands. The trouble was I had no idea where to aim—crewmen converged from all sides.

Then another ripping sound came from the bag, so loud that everyone paused to look. Wind tore through the slit I'd made, flowing into the superstructure, but no new rip had appeared.

Fritz had torn open the outer skin of the airship.

That's when I spotted the spy. He stood on a gangway above me, leaning against a bulkhead, as momentarily shocked as the rest of us.

Fortunately, I recovered more quickly.

I hit him in the leg, but with the Webley, that's all it took. The spy went down. I heard his gun clatter, dropped from his gangway into the bowels of the ship.

That got the legitimate crew moving. They rushed me.

One came between me and the tear I'd created. He grabbed for me, but I ducked and punched him hard in the gut. He stumbled into the railing.

"Sorry, must dash." I slipped past him, pirouetted on the gangway, and dove through the tear.

I fell about five feet before landing on a hovering disc-like platform. Before me stood von Drachen, wearing some kind of gas mask connected to a tank on his back. Behind and above him loomed Fritz, who was piloting us through the rip into the night sky. Rain pelted us from the dark.

The platform tilted as it slid free of the *R101*, forcing me to shift my balance. Von Drachen, already braced for this maneuver, aimed his strange gun at me, this time at my heart.

"You're a very persistent girl, Miranda." His voice still sounded muffled by the gas mask, though the words came clear enough. "A pity."

A lighting bolt blinded us both momentarily. He fired anyway. I ducked.

The beam scorched the air above me, and I returned fire. My bullet struck him full in the chest.

The impact knocked him into Fritz before he slumped to the deck. The robot seemed unperturbed by the death of its creator, so I spared a glance behind me.

The *R101* was burning. Von Drachen's strange ray had ignited the gasbag we'd vacated. The crew must have seen the platform in front of the airship, for I heard the bell ring for dead slow.

They might avoid us, but it wouldn't save them now. Already the fire had spread, unnaturally fast, fueled by hydrogen and whatever catalyst had been loosed by the gun. I felt the heat but a moment, for we soon left the airship behind us.

Metal creaked behind me, and I turned. Fritz had finally noticed von Drachen's death, apparently. It took a ponderous step towards me, giant arms outstretched.

Another flash revealed its face: cylindrical, featureless, save for a pair of sad blue eyes. Glass eyes, I realized, repurposed as actual organs of sight.

I shot it four times in the chest.

Von Drachen had been right. Fritz didn't even slow down.

It almost caught me, but I dove between its legs. Fortunately I'd bobbed my hair a few years back.

My shoes gripped the rain-slick deck as I crouched by von Drachen's body. I hoped his gun had landed nearby. If anything could stop this behemoth, that could. Unless, of course, it had fallen over the side.

I heard Fritz turn around behind me, slow but relentless as an oncoming train. I had precious little room to dodge, and only Fritz knew how to land the platform. Even if I could work out the controls in the dark, I'd never be able to reach them.

I shoved the Webley into my backpack and groped for the raygun.

Then came something extraordinary: the robot cried out, its voice deep, cold, and mournful. *"Tot! Mein Vater ist tot!"* A little boy, crying for his dead father.

Reaching for his killer.

Lightning flashed, showing how close Fritz stood. It also revealed the gun, off to my left.

Fritz grabbed at both of my legs, wanting perhaps to rip me apart. I leapt sideways in a *pas de chat*, scooped up the gun, spun, and fired.

I barely winged Fritz in the side, but its casing reddened and melted. With a final scream of tortured metal, Fritz toppled over the edge of the platform.

I had no time to celebrate, for the platform soon scraped against the tops of some trees. Determined to try the controls, I frantically searched for a way to reach them.

Another bolt lit up the sky, but this one struck the platform as well, causing it to spin like a discus. I fell unceremoniously onto my arse. The impact knocked the gun from my grasp. Helplessly, I heard it slide along the wet deck and fall noiselessly off the edge.

I cursed, crawling on hands and knees toward the edge myself.

Mere yards below flew the tops of trees. I had seconds before the platform crashed.

Mouthing a prayer for king and country, I leapt into the night.

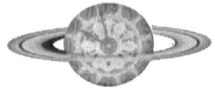

Cliff Winnig's fiction can be found in *Amberzine*, the *Footprints* anthology (Hadley Rille Books), and *Cinema Spec: Tales of Hollywood and Fantasy*. His nanofiction has appeared in the twitterzines *Outshine* and *Thaumatrope*. When not writing, he plays sitar, studies tai chi and aikido, and joins his wife Debby in social dancing, including ballroom, swing, salsa, and Argentine tango. Cliff has both flown in an airship and studied ballet, but not at the same time. He can be found online at http://cliffwinnig.com.

Dreams like Snowflakes

Todd Wheeler

Smoke drifted from beneath the Main Street Bridge in Waltham. My friends and I stood where the embankment slid down to the Charles River. The snow was piled up high and we couldn't see who was under the bridge.

The Blizzard of '78 had dumped five feet of snow around Boston, closing the schools. I had been outside all day with Tara and David, and his younger brother Freddy. We built forts and had snowball fights, and got chased out of a parking lot by a snowplow driver. My feet were wet despite the plastic bread bags my mom made me wear over my socks. Can you imagine a 13-year-old these days wearing bread bags with their boots?

We all lived in the same apartment building and were heading home when we saw the smoke.

"Probably drunks and bums under the bridge," David said.

"Let's go down there and see," Tara said. She wore a powder blue coat and matching mittens, and a pink hat with a pom-pom. But she was tough underneath those pastel colors. She clenched her hands as if spoiling for a fight.

"No way. They'll kill you. Then they'll rape you." David stepped away from the embankment. I think David was born scared. He could run faster than anyone I knew.

"Chicken!" Tara turned her back on David and looked at me. "Kevin, you'll go with me, right?"

"You bet," I said.

"C'mon, Freddy." David pulled his brother after him. "We'll get in trouble if we're late for dinner."

"Awww," said Freddy.

David started walking across the bridge. Freddy stopped and launched the leftover ice balls he had in his pockets, the snow packed hard to maximize the pain. He had a strong arm for a little kid. Years later, he'd make it to the Cape Cod baseball league—even had a cup of coffee at spring training with the Red Sox. That was before his motorcycle accident, after which he never walked again.

I shielded Tara while she formed her own ammunition. She hit David in the face with a ball of slush.

"All right!" David said. "We surrender! Let's go, Freddy."

"Got him back for last summer," Tara said with a grin.

Last summer. We had hung out in the shade of our apartment building, a place other kids called the projects. Tara wore a rainbow colored bikini top and David had pulled loose the knot at her neck. It was a quick peek as her top fell, hardly saw a nipple. David got a bloody nose for that trick. And she obviously hadn't forgiven him yet.

I was angry as well. I knew David did it because he secretly liked Tara. But I did too and wished I had been the one to teach him a lesson.

Tara and I stepped down the embankment, holding onto trees bent heavy with snow. The foul water of the Charles River was frozen over. Even when the river was high in the spring, there was a dry strip of sand under the bridge. There, as David said, rough looking men would hang out and drink. They'd smash their bottles against the bridge piers and leave piss and condoms and worse in their wake.

Tara and I edged around the snow bank, following the white thread of smoke that smelled like Christmas. Under the bridge, a kid who looked our age squatted over a small fire, warming his hands. His short hair was dyed white and shaved into a mohawk. He wore a black leather jacket, ripped jeans and dirty sneakers.

"Wassup," I said.

"My name is Morozko." His voice had a slight accent. "But you can call me Mike. Want a drink?"

He offered a pint in a brown paper bag. It tasted like vodka and burned our throats. We introduced ourselves, talked about the snow and school being out.

"School will teach you nothing," Mike said.

"What do you do?" Tara asked.

"I wander, letting the world provide my lessons. I walked to here from Boston."

"Yeah right," I said.

"It does not take long on the river. I will show you."

Mike took another swig from the bottle and stepped onto the ice. He held the pint out, beckoning to Tara. She followed, shot me her 'dare you' eyes. Shit, I was usually the ringleader; I couldn't back down. I thought for sure we'd crack through to the foul sludge below. They'd find us drowned, pinned under the ice or swirling near the dam in Watertown.

It got dark under the bridge. My vision went fuzzy. Mike

appeared to recede into a tunnel. Did he spike the alcohol? One leaden step at a time, I pushed on, watching Mike and Tara get farther away. Wind rushed in my ears and I felt pinpricks of ice on my cheeks.

And then I was on the other side of the river. The ice was solid, not a hole or crack to be seen. I could see my footprints all the way across. Tara's steps went halfway then stopped. There was no trace of Mike, not even the fire.

Did Tara ditch me, playing a trick with her new friend? I searched both sides of the bridge. They had disappeared like a breath in the cold air. As I walked home, I wondered if I had gone crazy, if it had even happened.

My mother worked the late shift. It was just me and her. My Dad left years ago for Florida to gamble and drink. He would call on my birthday and ask if I could loan him money.

I let myself into the apartment and changed out of my wet clothes, trying to decide what to do. In a cast-iron pan, I cooked a Steak-umm. Remember Steak-umms? They were thin pieces of processed beef, the only thing I knew how to make besides a peanut butter sandwich. At the kitchen table, I chewed the white bread and meat, not tasting it, not seeing anything but that kid, Mike. It was his eyes that bugged me: cold and blue like sapphires.

The year before, 1977, had been the year of serial killers. Ted Bundy had escaped from prison. Son of Sam terrorized New York. The Hillside Strangler roamed Los Angeles. David's words ran around my brain. They'll kill you, then they'll rape you. I had to look for Tara again.

In the corner of the hall closet was a toolbox, the only thing my

Dad left when he moved out. I took the claw hammer and stuck it in my belt behind my back.

Next stop was Tara's apartment, just to make sure she hadn't ditched me and was home now, laughing about it. Her mother cracked the door a few inches. She looked drunk. Tara said she was often drunk. Behind her, the boyfriend sauntered up in his sleeveless t-shirt, beer in one hand and cigarette in the other.

Tara's older sister, Megan, had split last year. Tara said the boyfriend had punched Megan. Or maybe he had *hit* on Megan. Tara wasn't home, I was told. I knew I had to save Tara from that kid Mike. But really I wanted to rescue her from much more than that.

Last stop was David's apartment.

"Davey's eating his dinner," his mother said.

His parents were old. When I first met them, I thought he lived with his grandparents. Couldn't imagine how Freddy was born. And his parents were strict. His father would beat David with a belt for any reason, or no reason at all. I could see David inside, waving his hand for me to get the hell out. I made our code sign, a two finger salute, to meet me behind the apartment building. An hour later, he found me shivering in the dark woods along the Charles. I explained the problem.

"I'm not going under the bridge," David said.

"Okay, don't. Just back me up. I'll go first and if there's trouble, you take off. Get the cops or something."

As we got close to the bridge we could see a light coming from beneath. David surprised me by going all the way in. There was Mike again, squatting by the fire. Tara stood nearby.

"Welcome back," Mike said.

"You okay?"

Tara's skin was pale in the light, her lips blue, her eyes glassy. Something was really wrong. Had he drugged her? And then David pushed past me, stumbling as if he walked through slush. Mike smiled and touched David's forehead. David's skin went pale, his eyes glazed and staring. I pulled the hammer out from underneath my coat.

"I'm going to mess you up bad," I said.

But I couldn't. I had looked at Mike's eyes and now I was frozen. I fought it, trying to will that hammer down towards Mike. He smiled, rubbing his hands.

"Even I get a chill sometimes. It is good to be with people whose desires burn in their souls. It melts the frost from my heart."

"What—" I tried to say.

"What do I want? Nothing. I have all that I need. I have seen the world cold and dead, and also full of life. When the ice sheet retreated, I had to stay up north. It has been ages since I have traveled in these parts. A long time since so much snow was here." Mike sidled up to Tara, stroked her cheek with his bony fingers. "I do not need anything. The question is: what do you want?"

"I—" Tara started.

"No!" I said, the effort making me tired, sleepy. I knew Mike was trouble, was going to cause us trouble.

"I want...to be pretty," Tara said.

That struck me as crazy. Sure, Tara didn't have breasts popping out of her velour shirt like Norma at school. Or a smile like Wendy's that could get a boy to do whatever she wanted. But Tara was pretty. I thought she was pretty. Mike nodded, grinning, his teeth sharp like icicles.

"I want to be better than my brother!" David blurted out.

Who were these kids? I felt like I had never met them, never spent time with them. How had I missed the insecurities of my friends?

I understand it now, how we had held back our hurts from each other, convinced no one else felt the same way. Convinced we were all alone. Back then under the bridge, hearing us speak our dark wishes, it was as if we were separated by a narrow, deep crevasse: close to each other but unreachable.

"What do you want, Kevin?"

I struggled not to speak. I could see nothing but Mike's eyes boring into mine. Cold, hard, blue eyes. Like my father's.

"I want you to die," I said, swinging the hammer.

But he wasn't there, of course. The fire was gone, just a little light from the moon by which to see. We twisted around in confusion as we looked for Mike. David panicked and ran. I tried to hold Tara, to warm her up I told myself. She pushed me away, tears running down her face. I walked home alone.

Ever look back at those times and ask, "How'd we survive?" We didn't wear helmets, barely wore seatbelts. No hand warmers or Gore-Tex coats. Just plastic bread bags to keep our feet dry. We stumbled through days mundane and magical, dreams of our future like snowflakes on the windowpane.

I saw David at our 20th high school reunion. He had a gut and a hairpiece, and showed me pictures of his kids. He said Freddy was doing well, a great wheelchair racer. The family was proud of Freddy for doing something with his life. I wondered how David had become so old so fast.

Tara got her wish. She was pretty in high school, and hung out with the popular kids. We dated once, but she said it wouldn't work. She had ambition and said I didn't, that I'd never leave the projects where we grew up. Broke my heart.

Tara became a model, lived fast in New York City. They found her one morning in a dumpster, overdosed on heroin, track marks between her toes.

I live in Las Vegas. At the poker table, I win more than I lose. Except when I don't. When my father died last February, his brother shipped the body to Boston. My mother went to the funeral. I told her I couldn't go. Too damn cold in February. I don't ever want to see snow again.

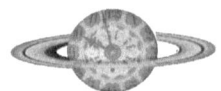

Todd Wheeler is a writer of speculative fiction who swears that everything in his story is true—except for the parts he made up. His stories have appeared in online and print venues, including *Atomjack Magazine*, *On the Premises*, and the anthology *Sporty Spec: Games of the Fantastic*. Each year he runs a virtual Summer Reading Program to benefit library and literacy charities. Additional information about him and his writing can be found at http://todd-wheeler.com.

Zeb

Karen A. Romanko

The seventies. Disco was hitting a crescendo and everyone went out to the clubs. Yeah, we loved to do the hustle, but what we really wanted was to meet guys. Back then you didn't go without a boyfriend for too long—your Mama started to worry.

We disco dollies floated into Flicks, a club in Boston, the usual scene—Huckapoo shirts on top of double-knit slacks accented by reflected, mirrored lights.

I hadn't made it past the threshold, when he asked me to dance. He looked young, but he was cute, so I said yes.

His name was Zeb, a name you didn't hear much. We had sweet, umbrella-covered drinks and chatted like old friends for the rest of the evening. He was unusually attentive, and late in the night he held my hand.

As the club closed, he asked if he could drive me home. Now my friends and I had a strict rule—always go home with the girls you came with—but Zeb was nice, so I said yes.

As we drove home, I started to squirm. What was I thinking? This man was a complete stranger, not to mention taking a route I'd never travelled—and, yeah, there was something a little off about his eyes. His hands were unnaturally cold too.

But as the minutes passed, and familiar highway signs appeared, I relaxed. The swift, smooth ride was soothing, and we talked lazily. Finally he said, "I'm out of cigarettes. Do you mind if we stop?"

As we pulled up to the convenience store, he asked me to go inside. "A pretty girl shouldn't sit alone in a car," Zeb said.

We entered the store, and he headed straight for the back, now in search of munchies, he said. When I looked up from the magazine rack, he was gone.

I ran out to look for the car—it was parked on the dark side of the store. That's when I saw the spaceship. It looked like a red '73 Mustang, but since I had never known a Mach 1 to hover above the ground, I knew it was a spaceship.

Zeb grabbed me from behind and tried to slip a smelly handkerchief over my mouth. Bad idea. I elbowed him in the abdomen and flipped him over my shoulder like a life-sized Raggedy Andy. When I looked at him on the ground, he was passed out cold.

Then things got weird. The hatch/door of the spaceship/Mustang opened and a man walked out. The man looked exactly like Zeb. Zeb II took one look at Zeb I, lying splayed on the asphalt, and ran back inside his little red ship. The vehicle ascended, leaving Zeb The First prostrate at my feet.

Zeb came to a few minutes later.

"So what's with the shiny ship and the identical twin?" I asked.

"I didn't want you for sex, really," Zeb said.

"I'm flattered."

"It's not that," he said, pulling himself more upright against the brick wall. "Sex between your species and mine doesn't work, take my word for it. I was just looking for a little companionship. We're a little short on females where I come from."

"And the clone?"

"We patterned ourselves after someone named 'Greg Brady' on your television transmissions, but we made a few modifications as a safety precaution."

"Oh, yeah, I can see it now. I used to have a crush on Greg Brady."

"Are you going to call the authorities?"

"Well, Zeb, I did make a phone call, but it was to the cab company. The police? I don't think so. I can picture it now. 'Mom, Dad, I caught a ride home from the club with an extraterrestrial, and he tried to abduct me.' Dad will have me moved out of my apartment and back in my old room before you can say 'Gort, Klaatu barada nikto.' Of course, you might actually succeed in abducting a woman in some accidental, Barney Fife-kind of way, but that's not my problem. There's my cab. Goodnight, Zeb from the planet Whatever. Don't show up at Flicks again."

He didn't, although I suppose I might not have noticed, if he'd changed his appearance. Still, I kept my eyes peeled for ersatz David Cassidys and Peter Framptons.

I don't know if the typical alien abduction story—bright lights in the desert, being zapped into a spaceship—is true. But I do know you should be wary of men in clubs who buy you drinks and ply you with sweet talk, especially if they offer to drive you home in a Mustang.

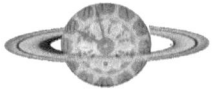

Karen A. Romanko has seen over 100 of her poems and short stories published in venues such as *Strange Horizons*, *Aberrant Dreams*, *Ideomancer*, and *The Pedestal Magazine*. She is editor of two speculative fiction and poetry anthologies, *Sporty Spec: Games of the Fantastic* (2007) and *Cinema Spec: Tales of Hollywood and Fantasy* (2009), both from Raven Electrick Ink. "Zeb" received an Honorable Mention in the *AlienSkin Magazine* "Science Fiction Good Writing Contest" in 2006.

Ticktock Girl

Cat Rambo

The reporter leans forward. "I understand you were actually built in 1895, and after your creator passed away, spent a number of years in storage. Can you tell us a little bit about that?"

And so she remembers.

Moment 20244660: She sits in the front parlor, covered with white cloth. Subdued spring light washes through the folds each afternoon. Behind her in the cavernous room, the *tick tock* of the grandfather clock echoes, counterpointed by the steps of the servant come to wind it. The maid must be accompanied by a girl in training today; they speak in quiet, subdued tones, bringing with them the smell of soap and lemon oil.

"Spooky, that's what it is. 'Ow long has it all sat here?" The voice is high-pitched, shot through with a nervous giggle.

"Since her ladyship died. Her father ordered it all covered up, and it's sat here ever since. Going on ten years now."

"What's this now?" The dusty sheet, tugged by an inquisitive hand, slides off her face and the new maid lets out a shriek of surprise before she is quieted by the older one.

"That's the lady's mechanical woman. Used to walk and talk, they say. Still can. But her lordship said, sit here, and so she does." With a deft rustle, the sheet is tucked around her again, but as the light dims, she preserves the sight of wide blue eyes, a mouth agape in astonishment.

"Walk an' talk? Go on, yer pulling me leg."

"That's what they say. Used to march alongside her in the suffrage parades."

A cog, imprisoned in her brain, ticks, and she enters a new moment, this one left behind.

Humans see time as a flow. A river, sweeping them along. But she perceives each moment, each tick and tock of the clock as a separate instance, presented as perfect as a gem inside a velvet box, each distinct minute collected within the celluloid and circuitry of her brain.

Moment 1: There is something hot and hard hammering inside her chest, but perhaps that is ordinary. She has no other moments to compare this one with, here and now in the first sixty seconds of life. All that exists is the face hovering above her where she lies on a table. The features are flushed with triumph and perspiration, a mass of golden brown ringlets falling around it, one touching her brass skin.

The lips open, and sounds come out. They have meaning attached to them. "Can you hear me?"

Her own lips move. The rubber bags that are her lungs contract, squeezing out air for her tongue to shape. "Yes."

Water appears on her skin. In some other moment she will know these are Sybil's tears, but not tears of sorrow, tears of joy. There will be many kinds of tears.

"I am Lady Sybil Fortinbras," the face says. "I am your creator."

Then, with a laugh, "Creatrix, I suppose."

The moment ends before she can reply.

Moment 25153800: The smell of seawater and musty cargo crates, part of so many moments, is gone. There is a long slow screech as each nail is withdrawn.

Moment 25153804: The lid comes off, and around her the packing material rustles as someone throws handfuls of it aside. Then her face is cleared and she sees him, hears his voice saying in German, "A woman? What use is a mechanical woman to me? *Schiesse!*" He throws the last handful back and she watches it drifting down in slow motion, settling to block her sight again.

Moment 8820967: They are marching in a suffrage parade. Along High Street, hostile faces loom, shouting. She wheels Lady Sybil's chair forward. Both of them wear white dresses, sashes of purple and green. Purple for courage, green for strength. The other women ignore her. She makes them uneasy, even though she may be the only reason the crowd doesn't rush to attack them. But one, her face lean and resolute as a hatchet, leans forward to speak to Lady Sybil.

"Do you agree with what Mrs. Pankhurst says?"

Lady Sybil glances up impatiently amid the sea of white ruffles. "That the argument of the broken pane is the most valuable argument in modern politics? Perhaps. But we will work within the law. For now." Her eyes are shrewd as she looks at the people lining the street. "Why would we want the vote if we intend to go outside the bounds of the law?"

Moment 9097372: Lady Sybil is speaking. The winter has withered her even more. She is frail and fragile as a songbird.

"You see, I don't think it's enough to march anymore," she says. "There has to be some good coming from you. In this brave new age, there are villains aplenty. I'll set you after them. You have been my legs, my dear. My mechanical Athena. For so very long. And now you will be my fists."

Moment 9156658: She has the dark-skinned, well-dressed man by the collar, pulling his limp form after her into the offices of Scotland Yard. She drops him in the doorway of Todd Chrisman, the detective who, she knows, has been working on the case.

"This is the Maharishi of Terjab," she says.

His eyes are amazed. "Yes, I can see that."

"He is responsible for the Soho white slave ring. You will find the evidence in his basement."

He stammers out something, moves forward to look down at the Maharishi. "What are you?" he says.

"Lady Fortinbras's mechanical Athena," she says. "My directive is to fight evildoers."

Behind him in the office, someone laughs, only to be hissed into silence by a fellow. All of these men are watching her.

✳ ✳ ✳

Moment 9230101: "This is the Dog Collar Killer," she says to Chrisman.

The man at her feet groans, recovering himself. He fought hard.

"He's a clergyman," Chrisman says, astonishment coloring his voice.

Pallid and rabbity, the man wears his robes like a squatter moved into a strange new place. He blinks, the bruises along his face coloring like dark water, and one eye weeps bloody tears.

"I am Father Jeremiah, and this is an outrage," he says, pulling himself upward despite the restraining hand on his arm.

"Marilyn Bellcastle," she says. "Lucy Stipe. Annabel Jones. He killed them all."

He explodes in spittle and anger at the sound of her voice. "Whores!" he snarls. "Jezebels! They deserved no better!"

Moment 9618905: "What have you brought us now, lass?" Chrisman asks. She gives him the papers she has compiled, the blueprints for the bomb to be placed beneath the Houses of Parliament and he thanks her, riffling through the rustling papers one by one, studying them. There are new decorations on his uniform; her aid has brought him a promotion.

Moment 9713637: Lady Sybil's father paces up and down the study, talking to himself. His cooling breakfast, the opened letter beside it, sits on the table. He wheels on her.

"Died in prison, by god!" he shouts. "Her and that Pankhurst woman, thinking hunger strikes would change the gaolers' minds. What good is it dying for a stupid, frippery cause, just another chance to dress up?"

She believes this is a rhetorical question; she makes no reply. She would have been with them, but Lady Sybil felt chasing the Ghost of Belfast was more important. Chrisman should have been pleased when she brought the villain in, but he was subdued, told her simply to go home.

"I'll have every man in that prison to court," Lord Fortinbras says. He looks at her, the way he has always looked at her. Half repulsed and half proud at his clever daughter's creation.

"And you, mechanical Athena," he says. "What's to become of you now?"

There are tears on his face.

Moment 25055955: The crack of the gavel resounds through the crowded room as the auctioneer bangs the sale closed. "And sold to the foreign gentleman!"

Some of Lady Sybil's friends are there, but none of them have bid on her. She is led away to the waiting crate. She feels nothing.

Moment 49189954: Professor Delta is speaking.

"The university bought you as a historical feminist treasure," she says. "Built by an English suffragette and scientist. The 'once owned by Hitler' stuff, that was just icing on the cake, a little thrill value. But now…nowadays people are more concerned with the rights of mechanicals than they were when you were sold."

There is a gleam in her eye that is reminiscent of the Pankhursts.

"Do you really want to be on your own?" Delta says, leaning forward. She is a short, wiry woman, her hair cropped close, no makeup on her face. "What would you do?"

"Fight crime," she says.

Delta leans back, her hand flickering in a dismissive gesture. "A superhero? Let the papers call you something like Ticktock Girl? How...trivial. It would be a terrible waste."

She could go back in the crate. But Lady Sybil built her to move. To act. To be her hands, even now.

Moment 57343680: She faces Father Jeremiah in the closed room, cinderblock walls, the smell of disinfectant harsh and immediate. Somewhere in the distance, water drips.

She's not sure how he can be alive, unchanged, a century later. But here he is.

"The Lord has preserved me! I am his Hand!" he shouts at her. She calculates the distance from her fist to his jaw, the amount of impact necessary to render him unconscious.

He draws himself up and smiles. "But you can't. I'm legit now."

The word is unfamiliar.

He splits it into syllables for her, serves it up like little rabbit pellets of words. "Le-gi-ti-mate. Everything I do is inside the law."

"You tell people to kill other people and they do it."

"All I do is provide information on where they are: the

abortionists, the sodomites, the women who whore themselves out. My followers decide what to do with the knowledge."

Seeing her pause, he laughs. "Welcome to the brave new world, Ticktock, mechanical clock," he half sings. "Can't touch this, can't touch me now."

Moment 9097375: Sickness has eaten away at Lady Sybil's face, reducing it to paper over bone. But her voice is strong as ever.

"There is right and there is wrong," she says. "You, my mechanical Athena, are always on the side of right." A trembling hand strokes along the bright metal of her face. "The side of justice."

Moment 57343681 seems to blend together with so many others, so many long circles of the wheels in her brain. And in that confluence, she knows that sometimes the argument of brick and fist is the only way. Chrisman would not approve, she thinks as she snaps Jeremiah's neck. But Lady Sybil would.

Cat Rambo's work has appeared in such places as *Asimov's*, *Weird Tales*, and *Strange Horizons*. Her collection *Eyes like Sky and Coal and Moonlight* appeared in 2009, following her collaboration with Jeff VanderMeer, *The Surgeon's Tale and Other Stories*, in 2007. She is the managing editor of online publication *Fantasy Magazine*, http://www.fantasy-magazine.com. She likes superheroes.

"Ticktock Girl" first appeared in *Cyber Age Adventures*, September 2005.

All That Remains Is the Middle

Lon Prater

Decmber 26, 1928

To my godson Edwin J. Theodore,

There are such women, such loves, capable of stopping the march of time around a man, of moving him beyond reach of the clock's clawed hands, if only for a while. As I write this, I am near the end of my life; which has been long and happy, despite the seemingly short distance between the dates of my actual birth and death. (But I am getting ahead of myself, as the phrase goes.)

In a way, I am writing this brief memoir as much to relive my earliest and best memories as I am to preserve them with you when my life is over. Above all, I'm writing this letter to beg you, *beg you* to seize love with both hands when she appears to you, and treasure every moment you share with her.

That is the choice I made, and it was because of a letter such as this one that I did so.

"Uncle Ted" was no true uncle of mine, though he had been welcomed into our family over the course of a long and successful business relationship with my father. Long after my parents passed away (Mother with scarlet fever, Father of the consumption), Uncle Ted remained a regular though somewhat aloof fixture in my life. Being a solitary type, I was married to the business of managing my inheritance and devoted most of my time and thought to making it multiply, much as you are now. Over the years after Father passed, Uncle Ted and I drifted apart. Near the end of his life, we only saw each other at Christmas and Thanksgiving.

Except for one slate grey day in the last December of his life when he brought a picture to my doorstep. It was a beautiful girl with lustrous black hair and an imp's smile peeking out from an hourglass shaped locket. "Have you ever seen such a beauty? Such an enchantress as my—" said he, the thick bristles of his mustache and beard quivering with excitement as he spoke. But he broke off, eyes wide as if he were surprised at his own words.

I replied quite honestly that I had not. He seemed perturbed with himself, and overly willing to let the conversation shift to other things. We drank port and smoked cigars for some time after, discussing Wall Street and the erratic nature of the market. After a time, the old man wandered out into the night and summoned a horseless buggy to take him home.

So it took me a bit by surprise to see him a few days later as I was riding downtown to the tailor, speaking to the exact same girl whose picture he had shown me in a locket but a few nights before. Did I say speaking? Sobbing at her is more accurate. His timeworn face was twisted up in the most heartrending way, and she—this angel of innocence and beauty, this muse to the Gods—she was listening to him attentively, and fingering the self-same hourglass locket at her throat. Though I later determined what was said to the girl, it isn't something I feel at ease repeating here. (I trust that if you ever find yourself in a similar situation, you will exercise the same discretion.) I only saw them for a moment before they were swept away in the rush of foot traffic, and I went on about my day's business of ordering new suits for the new year.

My investments continued to prosper despite some odd swings in the preceding months, and that Christmas I invited Uncle Ted over for an especially celebratory dinner, as had become our tradition. Flush with recent success, I boasted to him that once Hoover got into office, the market would only grow stronger. He tutted me softly and refused to speak of Wall Street, turning his attention to the ham instead.

By way of making conversation, I asked him (somewhat awkwardly, I admit) about the lovely creature from the locket, mentioning having seen the two of them on the street. His eyes went wide momentarily and he swallowed the food in his mouth without chewing it any further. "I no longer have the locket," he said. "I've given it back to her."

Astonished, I asked him why he would do such a thing, but he would not answer. I assumed it was a matter of a randy old man being discrete about his young mistress and pursued it no further. Our discourse for the rest of the meal went clumsily and when he left that night, he took great pains to show his gratitude and affection, even hugging me firmly goodbye in lieu of his usual steel-trap handshake.

All in all, his manner seemed to indicate that we would never see each other again. Which turned out to be both true and untrue, to varying degrees, as I'm sure you are beginning to understand.

Uncle Ted froze to death that late December night. I found him on my porch, pace marks showing where he had exercised a brutal force of will as even to the end he refused to knock and be let in to the warmth of my home. Choosing to die like this, cold and alone...You will find it hard to understand, I know; but in time you'll doubtless come to see why he chose to do it, why I chose to do it, and why you'll choose to do so as well, when the time comes.

Without question, you are now wondering just how batty your godfather (and namesake, don't forget!) truly was, writing an extraordinary letter like this and leaving it for you to find in his frozen hands on your doorstep the morning after Christmas. For the poor courtesy of it all, not to mention the sorrow and incomprehension of sudden loss you're feeling, I offer my humblest and most heartfelt apologies.

At some point, you will come to understand that by arranging my demise in this way, and preparing this letter for you, I have done all that I could to set you on the path to a happy and fulfilling life. Even now, from the vantage of my hundred and twenty-odd years ('tis true!) I boggle at what I could tell you about what happened to me after I found that letter—this letter.

What I did, and what you must do, is abandon your bank statements and stock certificates and FIND THE GIRL! The one from the locket, I mean. She will be near the same corner where you saw me giving her back the locket. She will be waiting for you, just as she was waiting for me.

When you go to her, know this: she is no angel, but certainly no demon; she's something altogether different. She lives for love, and her love is a force strong enough to take a man outside of time, outside of himself even. Oh, if only it could have lasted!

But I will share a part of her mystery here. The most alluring part of Uncle Ted's letter, as I recall: she'll ask you one question before she puts her locket round your neck.

"Do you dare accept a love stronger than time itself?"

I can only tell you that I agreed, as you will, intrigued as only a career bachelor can be by such a captivating offer. Of what happens beyond the moment that locket of hers slips over your head and comes to rest on my shoulders, I can tell you only two things:

First, that she is true to her word. The nature of this delightful woman's affection is such that time literally slows down around the man lucky enough to be so well loved. I have lived to see *amazing* things so far into the future—well past the year 1990!—that even now I revel in the memories of them!

And second: When that love flickers out at last (as you must know by now it shall) the time that she stretched about you for so long will recoil like a band of rubber, snapping you body and soul into the late 1890s; nearly thirty years before this very day. I won't presume to tell you what our history—and future—will require from you at that time.

Ah, to be loved like that again...If only I were you once more, embarking on the adventure afresh. Not stamping and pacing and scrawling this letter on your porch by the light of the moon.

Go to her, Edwin. Go now, without hesitation or reservation. You've filled the lonely beginning of our life with numbers and news and money (soon to be worthless, you'll see!) while I've spent the end mourning the love I lost and waiting thirty years for this chance to reclaim it.

All that remains is the middle; the glorious middle!

And though I have gone to great pains in this letter to keep from you the grand details of your own impending life and love, I will tell you this, Edwin: I do not regret one moment of it; even now, as my breath is still steaming into the late December night and my old frozen legs and feet are becoming less and less a part of me.

I must close now. I think I remembered all I needed this letter to say. Actually, I'm quite certain of the fact.

With much fondness and perhaps a touch of envy,

E. Theodore James

"Uncle Ted"

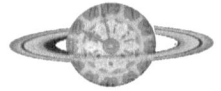

Lon Prater is an active duty Navy officer by day, writer of odd little tales by night. His short fiction has appeared in the Stoker-winning anthology *Borderlands 5*, *Writers of the Future XXI*, and Origins Award finalist *Frontier Cthulhu*. He is an avid Texas Hold'em player, occasional stunt kite flyer, and connoisseur of theme parks and haunted hayrides. To find out more, visit http://www.lonprater.com.

"All That Remains Is the Middle" first appeared in *Love and Sacrifice*, Zen Films Publishing, 2007.

Slipstream Fiction

Don D'Ammassa

O rdinarily, I don't pick through other people's garbage, but I was taking a roundabout route home to avoid the congestion on the highway and I ended up getting lost. Stubbornly, I refused to turn around and go back to familiar territory. Instead I pushed on, figuring that if I went far enough north, I'd run into the bend in the river and then any left turn should bring me back to the highway.

The neighborhood was nondescript but well maintained. It was trash day and blue recycling bins and black trash bags were arranged in little piles along both sides of the street. The houses were old, set well back from the road, probably not expensive when they were first put up but pricey now because of their proximity to the university. I reached the end of one block where I just happened to glance at the nearest pile of trash. There was the usual assortment, but on one side was a cardboard carton filled with books.

Yeah, that's my weakness. I pulled over to the curb and got out to investigate. A quick pass of the visible titles was unenlightening, but they seemed to be in good condition so I figured I could sort through them later, and put the whole box in the back seat. If worse came to worst, I'd donate them to a library book sale.

The next half hour was a series of frustrations verging on minor trauma. I found myself on an unmarked dead end street and had to back up a block to get out. Then I turned onto an avenue that curled around on itself and left me headed in the wrong direction.

As you can imagine, my shortcut ended up taking a lot longer than if I'd just gritted my teeth and stayed on the highway. By the time I got home I was in a foul mood, and I completely forgot about the books until the next day. It was early evening when I finally carried them inside.

Although the dust jackets were missing, they were in excellent condition. A little dusty, but no fading or discoloration, torn pages or broken spines, and not a hint of mustiness. They were by a variety of authors, several of whom had familiar names. I took them all out of the box and arranged them in piles, booted up my PC, and decided to check to see if I had any gems.

The first was a novel by Kenneth Roberts. I've read *Rabble in Arms* and *Northwest Passage*, so I was particularly curious about this one. It was titled *Wilderness Warriors* and had been published in 1938 by Kennebunk Press. There was no listing for it anywhere, not even on eBay. I set it aside and picked up the next.

The Ocean Full of Bowling Balls by J.D. Salinger was dated 1947 and had been published by Bagnell & Watson. There was a bookplate inside the cover, but the space left for the name was blank. I couldn't find any listing for this one on the internet either. The same was true for *Three More Lives* by Gertrude Stein, *The Road to Ruin* by F. Scott Fitzgerald, and *Those Days of Glory* by John Dos Passos. There were three books in nearly identical bindings all labeled Suspense House, obviously mystery novels. *Body on the Doorstep* was a Bencolin mystery by John Dickson Carr, *The Late Lamented Liar* by Raymond Chandler featured Philip Marlowe, and

Dorothy Sayers's *The Duke Is Dispatched* was subtitled "Lord Peter's Revenge." No hits on Google for any of them. There were at least a dozen more, but you get the idea.

One or two oddballs I could accept, but an entire box of them stretched my credulity. There were several different publishers, but when I tried searching for them, I got zero results.

I picked four books and took them to Cellar Stories in Providence. The owner looked them over, frowned, went to his computer, frowned some more, asked me where I'd gotten them. I lied and said a yard sale. He asked if I could leave them with him for a few days but I declined. His perplexity confirmed my own.

I went looking for the house where I'd found them and, as you can probably guess, I couldn't find it. I tried to retrace my steps, but a lot of the intersections looked very much alike. I waited until it was trash day on the East Side again and spent most of that morning driving up and down the streets, but no second box appeared, or if it did, I missed it.

I went home and, for the first time, actually picked up one of the books and started to read it. This might seem odd, that I waited so long, I mean, but there was an air of unreality about the whole thing, as though they weren't really there, or weren't really books. It was an intangible barrier that I had to force myself to penetrate.

The Chandler was the first. I like Chandler and I've read several of his novels. This one wasn't as good as *The Long Goodbye* or *The Big Sleep*, but it was still pretty good and it felt like a Chandler. I'm not as fond of Sayers but I tried her next. This one was set late in Wimsey's life. He and Harriet Vane had a daughter, and the daughter came home one day and told them she'd seen two men forcing a woman into an automobile. The story quickly became more convoluted and my attention strayed a bit, but it sure felt like Dorothy Sayers.

I went to bed reading *Wilderness Warriors*.

I suspected an elaborate hoax. Maybe back in the early 1940s, someone with more money than judgment commissioned these novels and had them printed privately. They might even be real novels by other writers, in some cases slightly rewritten to pass as "lost" novels. Yeah, that's quite a stretch, but you try coming up with a viable, non-fantastic explanation.

The second possibility was that somehow the books were authentic, but not from our reality, although I could not imagine how they had come here. I hadn't noticed anything anomalous in the books I'd read, but there might have been subtle differences that I just hadn't seen. Maybe they had materialized in an attic and someone had thrown them out without knowing what they were.

In any case, what could I do with them? If I tried to pass them off as authentic, I'd be lucky if I was just shown the door. Fraud charges were more likely. I thought about copying them into my computer, but Sayers and Roberts and Faulkner didn't have computers. There was no way I could print out a properly aged manuscript even if I could think of a way to explain how I had acquired these precious, lost works of fiction. I had the possibility of a fortune sitting in my living room, with no way to convert it into actual money.

One of the books was a collection of short stories, among which was a Sherlock Holmes mystery by Sir Arthur Conan Doyle. I retyped and printed it out. Four months later I had four rejection slips, but by then I'd finished retyping *Wilderness Warriors*. The first place I sent it returned the manuscript unread because they weren't considering unsolicited submissions. So I decided to get an agent, but four in a row told me that big historical novels didn't sell and, anyway, "due to the current market conditions, we're not taking on new clients at this time."

By then I'd finishing transcribing the Marlowe, changing his name to Dirk Chandler, but to my dismay NO significant publisher would look at unagented detective fiction either. Frustrated, I pushed the carton of books to the back of a closet and tried to forget about them.

A few months later Eblis Manufacturing decided that my department was overstaffed, and, since I had the least seniority, I found myself mailing resumes and collecting unemployment. With too much time on my hands, I dug out the box and started work on the Fitzgerald.

It was pretty much the same story. Most publishers didn't have time to look at work by an unknown (!!!) writer, and those who did suggested that I adopt a more contemporary style. One of them even wrote that the novel would have been appropriate during the Jazz Age, but that it didn't satisfy present day sensibilities. In desperation I turned to the small press, and nearly three years after I first retrieved that damned box of books, I received a letter accepting *The Road to Ruin* for publication. No advance, of course, but I would be paid double the industry standard royalty on actual sales.

Needless to say, I wasn't overjoyed. Not only was I not being paid, I didn't even have the satisfaction of seeing my work in print. Because it wasn't my work. It was word for word the work of F. Scott

Fitzgerald, or at least of one F. Scott Fitzgerald. Even so, I did feel a sense of accomplishment when a carton of advance copies showed up on my doorstep. I put them in the closet with the Sayers and Dos Passos and all the rest and decided to forget about them.

To my surprise, the book was a success. It was mostly word of mouth at first, and some favorable reviews on the internet didn't hurt. My publisher, Hayloft Press, went to a second, third, and then a much larger fourth printing. It was picked up by the chain stores, it threatened to sneak onto bestseller lists, and Hayloft wanted to know if I had anything else in the works. So did Simon & Schuster, Random House, and several other publishers. I sent the Roberts novel to one, the Sayers to another, and the Dos Passos to a third but each and every one came back with letters that said, basically, hey, where's the next Jazz Age novel.

I finally decided it wasn't worth the effort. I had made enough on the Fitzgerald to keep me in wine and cookies for at least a couple of years and maybe the situation would have changed by then. Maybe there'd be a sudden wave of interest in Gertrude Stein pastiches; the *Three Lives* centennial was only a couple of years away. In the meantime, I've found a new job and *The Road to Ruin* has just been optioned by Warner Brothers, so I have few complaints.

The mail came today as it usually does. I was outside trimming the shrubs near the front door when the truck pulled up. I exchanged casual remarks with the mailman, then sorted through circulars, bills, and magazines to see if my next royalty check was there. It wasn't, but there was a very neat looking envelope from somebody named "Di Filippo & Newton". The stamp commemorated the thirty-fourth President of the

United States, Estes Kefauver. I brought the mail inside, dropped the rest on an end table, and carefully peeled back the flap.

Inside was a two page letter, very formal, addressed to me and signed by someone named Michael Blake. The second page was a photocopy of a court filing. The first page informed me that the firm of Di Filippo & Newton was representing the estate of Frederick Scott Fitzgerald, and had been retained to initiate proceedings against me for copyright infringement, to wit, the reprinting of a work of fiction, *The Road to Ruin*, rights of which had been bequeathed to them by the aforesaid author and which were, as I must have known, covered by the copyright laws of these fifty-two United States of America.

I wonder how they plan to serve the subpoena.

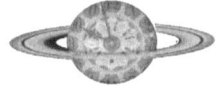

Don D'Ammassa is the author of seven novels, three reference books, and more than 100 short stories. He was book reviewer for *Science Fiction Chronicle* for twenty-five years and still reviews regularly on his website, http://dondammassa.com.

Putting off the Past

G. O. Clark

A new 3-way bulb in my reading lamp
lights the pages of this book about famous
poets who converged on Boston and Cambridge
in the Fifties and Sixties.

These are the mundane poets, a label
pinned upon them by some in the sci-fi field,
poets not truly hip to the future, though still
technically worthy of a close reading.

As stated, the locus of the book is Boston,
and its ivy league stations of the literary cross,
places I had little to do with when growing up
south of the city sprawl in a small town

along the train tracks, a town next to
the one where we buried my mother last spring,
the last of her generation, my sisters, cousins
and I growing older by the day.

I still haven't looked deep within to

write about her passing—or my father's—
a so called mundane poem lacking starships
and aliens and wonders of the future,

a future they did get a glimpse of when
Neal Armstrong stepped onto the moon, my mother
in the kitchen scrubbing all those pots and pans
of the moment, too busy to watch.

Instead I dip into this book in hand,
putting the day's regrets and worries on hold,
fingers flipping the pages instead of pecking at keys,
letting bottled up emotions go unchecked.

The new 3-way bulb replaces the more energy
efficient neon one, whose light seemed too cold and
sterile. It has an old fashioned warm glow, like
some memories of my past yet to be told.

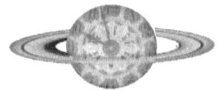

G. O. Clark's work has been published in *Asimov's Science Fiction*, *Talebones Magazine*, *Strange Horizons*, *Cinema Spec: Tales of Hollywood and Fantasy*, *The Rhysling Anthology*, and many other publications. He's the author of eight poetry collections, the two most recent being *Strange*

Vegetables (Dark Regions Press) and *Mortician's Tea* (Sam's Dot Publishing). He won the Asimov's Readers Award for poetry in 2001, and has been nominated twice for the Stoker Award. He retired from the University of California, Davis in 2008, where he worked in the library for many years. Visit Gary online at http://my.att.net/p/PWP-goclark.

The Fix

Marge Simon

It was 1940 and I was still a toddler when Greatgran came to live with us. I pretended later that she arrived in a bright blue Chevy Clipper, but I really don't remember. She was sitting at the breakfast table when I got up one morning. There were some large boxes and bags by the door. James Jr. took them upstairs when he got in from tending the flies. A couple of them were stuck to his face. Definitely a good omen.

"Toppy, this is your grandmother," said Momma. I didn't know what a grandmother was, but I was glad. Her dress went clear down to the floor and she was almost as tall as the door. There were purple sparkles around her head.

She had a copy of the first song recorded by Thomas Edison. It was called "Save a Little Dream for Me." I begged her to play it over and over on her old wind-up gramophone. I wish I'd been there for the very first record ever played but I was in the Waiting Time. I guess that's why I really liked it so much. During the Waiting Time you forget a lot of things you knew before. Then you get born and find out what you are supposed to be back for. Sometimes it's managing flies, like my brother, James Jr., does. Or the placement of trolls, or mending holes in the sky. That's how our family is.

Anyway, I was curious. I hung around her a lot even after I was old enough for school. I discovered she liked a small glass of brandy in the afternoon. This was when I was supposed to be taking a nap. Momma was on her exercise routine soaring East Mountain for an hour or so.

"I can't sleep, Greatgran. Would you tell me about Thomas Edison again? What is it really like to change history? How do you do that?"

"So many questions, little Toppy!" Greatgran took a sip of her brandy. She leaned back in the chair, smiling.

"Young Tom had too much going on," she said. "All I did was circle the one in his head that I wanted him to finish first." Seeing my blank look, she added, "Like your mother does with a grocery list. There's always something more important than anything else on it."

Then she told me how Tom Edison's mind was worse than some guy named Leonardo, when it came to finishing up ideas. "He would forget to eat. Didn't bathe regularly." She paused to shake her finger at me. "Mind you, Leo had a better handle on things. Very clean fellow, for the times. I do believe he would have invented a cologne for men, had I suggested it."

I guess that is so. I know she made him invent scissors. "Leo's greatest contribution," she'd say every time she took out her darning egg to mend a sock. Anyway, Momma came back and that was the end of our conversation.

I wasn't ever sure when Greatgran was busy dreaming history. She'd be sitting in her favorite Edwardian chair with her eyes closed, like she was napping. But Momma always knew whether it was a nap or a "fix," as she called it. Either way, she'd chase me outside to play. When I came in, there would be something new in the house. TV shows were suddenly in color. Plastic forks and spoons, frozen dinners. All you had to do was heat them up. They tasted nasty. I don't think Greatgran had anything to do with that one.

Once, I tried doing what she did. I climbed up into the Edwardian chair and closed my eyes.

I'd already decided whose mind I wanted to get inside. *Snow White* was my favorite movie. A man named Walt Disney made it up along with *Song of the South*. He was the best artist ever. I wanted him to make up a movie about Cinderella and I was sure he probably had that in his head. So that is who I was going to do a "fix" on.

I sat in that chair and concentrated hard as I could. The air became hard to breathe. Something terrible and dark slipped into my mind. It began to squeeze so I couldn't think. I didn't know what it was, but it couldn't be Walt Disney. I screamed. Next thing I knew, Greatgran was shaking me.

"Toppy! Wake up, child!" She knelt down to my level and looked hard in my eyes. "You've been trying a fix, haven't you. I should have known!"

"I'm sorry, Greatgran. Please don't be mad at me—" I started crying and she hugged me so hard it hurt. But it was a *good* kind of hurt. Then she picked me up and sat down herself, with me in her lap. "You had me very upset, Toppy."

"What was that awful thing in my head, Greatgran?" I asked.

Her eyes grew dark as violets. "There are things out there we can't see, child. Bad things. They live outside of time. Even *I* have to be careful when I am dreaming a change." She made me promise not to try this again. Of course I promised. But something deep inside told me I wasn't going to give up so easily, even if it was very dangerous. Anyway, after that Greatgran took me to the kitchen and gave me all the cookies I could eat. Imagine that! And it was only an hour until suppertime.

When I was nine, I just had to ask her. She was in the kitchen making tater bread. Her hands were measures for cups and tablespoons. There was a dust of flour in her hair. I sat on a stool watching her.

"Greatgran, what's it like when you're dreaming? How do you get inside people's heads to make them invent stuff?"

A strand of her hair had escaped its bun. She paused to blow it away, then looked at me. "Ah," she said. "You want to try it again, don't you." It wasn't a question. She always seemed to know what I was thinking.

"Please, Greatgran. please?"

"Toppy, child, she sighed, "it's something you won't learn until you're a lot older, so get that straight in your head. Even your mother can't do it. Takes practice." She turned back and started pounding down the dough. But not before I saw her smile.

So that's how I knew what I was here to do. Someday I'd be fixing up history like she did.

Just wait and see.

Marge Ballif Simon's works have appeared in *Chizine*, *The*

Pedestal Magazine, Strange Horizons, Flashquake, Dreams & Nightmares, and more. Her current collections include *Like Birds in the Rain* (Sam's Dot Publishing) and *Night Smoke*, with Bruce Boston (Kelp Queen Publications). Her self-illustrated poetry collection, *Artist of Antithesis*, was a finalist for the Bram Stoker Award in 2004. In 2008, she won the Stoker for Best Poetry Collection for *VECTORS: A Week in the Death of a Planet*, with Charlee Jacob. Marge is former President of the Science Fiction Poetry Association and serves as Editor of *Star*Line*.

The Last Time I Was in Vienna

Nancy Ellis Taylor

The last time I was in Vienna I had Hitler's head in my handbag and I was certain the Riesenrad, that giant Ferris wheel, was running again like the clockworks of a romance gone round and round and so slowly wrong. And I was certain as I looked up, I saw your face again, your smile waxing and waning like a jolly, sweet moon. I saw that smile again fade and form like the Cheshire Cat, all full of mysteries and hungry secrets. And I remembered there was something I needed to remember. This was after I had discovered absinthe but before the morphine. I remembered there was something I had missed. Like the taste of your kiss going around, around. Like the little knot of Trotskyites scuttling across the square. (Oh, you can always tell Trotskyites. Their eyes say, "I'm going to kill you!" But their eyebrows say, "I just want to be warm again.") They pushed me back, back into the rats and the rubble and in a little vulture swoop, grabbed my bag and ran and ran. I suspect they were looking for cigarettes. Petty revolutionaries always are, I suspect. And I remembered I was meant to be on a train to Paris. In the catacombs there are still Templar wardings and I remembered we were going to stop it all. We were going to crush that skull and hide the dust among the dead, never to unleash harm again. We. Mostly lost. Almost I see but the dreams cloud up and feel so much better that way. And now I hear that the center of evil sits somewhere south of St. Petersburg. (For me, forever St. Petersburg with my handprint in the snow and the samovar never empty. I will not invoke any other namings.) Evil sits, it does, in a drawer full of everything that is broken. I feel it waiting to be pulled, all innocent and accidentally, from the rubbish. And I am waiting, waiting to hear my name called out but I remember and suspect my courier days are over and I will never again know that kiss.

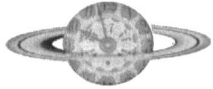

Nancy Ellis Taylor is an L.A.-based writer who gives readings locally several times a year. She is active with the Southland Poets of the Fantastic, a group devoted to science fiction, horror, and fantasy poetry, and Poets on Site, a local group which uses art in galleries and museums for poetic inspiration. Taylor has been a panelist, presenter, and reader on panels covering vampires, feminist POVs and poetry at Loscon. Samples of her work appear in a variety of online journals. Taylor is currently planning a collection of her L.A. poems.

U8: Alexanderplatz (1989)

C.D. Covington

After the Berlin Wall was built, stations in the East that served transit lines originating and ending in the West were closed off to prevent defection. People called them ghost stations.

Senior Sergeant Gerd Möller lit a cigarette and watched the subway train stop. The empty platform filled with people as schoolchildren waved to their friends and tourists stared at the signs directing them to the famous TV Tower next to Alexanderplatz, the station's namesake. Footsteps echoed through the tiled tunnel and up the stairwells.

As the train took off southward, the crowd on the platform faded, then vanished.

Underofficer Karl Bayer shivered, pallid under the fluorescent lights. "This happens every day?"

Möller drew on his cigarette and held it a moment before exhaling. "Most of them. Always between two scheduled U8 trains."

"Have you told the commander?" He wiped a bead of sweat off his forehead, hiding it in a straightening of hair.

"Of course. He laughed at me, said I was imagining things. I never could get anyone else to report it." Möller glanced at Bayer. Squared shoulders, polished boots, and a glint of enthusiasm in his new partner's eyes gave the impression of a *Mitarbeiter*, sent to make sure the man who sees invisible Western trains wasn't a dissident.

"What do you think it is?"

"The station."

"Sir?"

"Alex is giving us glimpses of what might be. I think he's lonely." He drew on his cigarette again. At the rattle of the real U8 on the track, he stood straighter.

Bayer snapped to attention, rifle at the ready, and glared sideways at Möller. When the train had passed, he said, "The station is lonely? Sir, that's..."

"Superstitious nonsense and ghost stories? That's what the commander said." He shrugged. "I thought so too, at first. Alexanderplatz isn't the only place I've seen these, you know." He paused a moment, to let Bayer cast a skeptical glance his way. When it didn't come, he continued. "I first saw a ghost train when I was sitting in a guardhouse above the tracks. Night shift, so the trains were far between. Quarter after midnight, this train comes by, and I call my captain on the radio. He says there's no train there. I spent the next day in confinement, learning not to drink on duty." Möller snorted. "I saw them once a week or so while I was out there. Alex wasn't always this active. Since Secretary Gorbachev introduced glasnost, he's been showing me his dreams more often."

Bayer's eyebrows rose. "You're talking as though the station is alive."

"All the souls that pass through here every day, and you think it isn't?" Möller took several steps away from Bayer and walked along the northbound tracks, scanning them up and down. Moments later, another ghost train pulled in, and people swarmed the platform, walking right through him. He spread his arms and touched a man's shoulder as he walked past.

Words formed on Bayer's lips, but they did not come. Fear flashed briefly before he fixed his façade. He stepped backward, dodging the ephemeral tourists. "Sir, don't you..."

They vanished, and Möller turned to face him. "Imagine it, Bayer. Kaiser Wilhelm built this station over a hundred years ago! How many people have passed through this tunnel? Even today, thousands of people pass under Alex's watchful eye."

"But it's only this platform that's closed. The other two lines through here are fully open." Bayer looked surprised that he'd made the argument and shook his head.

"True. He could be showing us scenes from the open tracks, as if to say the Wall we've built is nothing to him." He sat on one of the benches, its varnish peeling with decades of disuse, and faced the opposite track while a train rumbled northward. "Or that it will be nothing."

"Do you want the Wall to come down?" Neither Bayer's face nor voice betrayed any emotion.

Möller twitched his lips, amused. "You want me to give the Stasi a reason to lock me up?"

"I'm not Stasi," Bayer said smoothly.

Möller looked Bayer in the eyes. "You'd say that if you were. Want is a strong word. I think it's going to, whether I have any desires either way. Read the newspapers: reform is coming. How Honecker handles it is his own problem." He shrugged and crushed his cigarette butt under his boot. "I don't concern myself much with politics; I'm no revolutionary. I just do my job and follow orders."

"And imagine that a train station is alive." Skepticism tinged Bayer's voice, and his eyebrow lifted.

"You saw it, too. Do you have a better explanation?" A southbound train stopped and let out its passengers, the barren platform teeming with evanescent life.

Bayer shook his head. "There's no rational reason for it, but if I stay here long enough, I might start to believe it myself."

A sound like sighing came down the tracks, and the lights shone briefly brighter. "Alex is happy to hear that," Möller said.

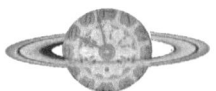

C.D. Covington's first German textbook had maps of a divided Germany and the words for bell-bottoms and reel-to-reel. Those maps were obsolete by the end of her first year of study, but Cold War-era Germany, especially Berlin, continued to intrigue her.

She earned a BS in chemistry and German from Juniata College and spent her junior year in Marburg, Germany. She lives in North Carolina and blogs at http://obligatedtoexaggerate.blogspot.com.

The Devil Went Down to the Sunset Strip

Dayle A. Dermatis

It was the conversation that every mother dreads having with her teenage daughter. The 80s were back in style, and I'd let her paw through an old box of my things for her Halloween costume. (Ouch.)

Then she came out of my bedroom holding a worn, torn black sweatshirt and a cassette tape and asked, "Mom, who's Angrrr Management?"

Crap. How was I supposed to answer that?

Could I be honest with her? Well, sweetie, they were an up-and-coming hair metal band and I was their groupie.

Or the full truth: Also, I saved the idiots from selling their souls to the Devil.

I slid into the curved, red-leather-covered booth next to Stixxx. (He was so proud of that nickname. They all had ones with triple letters to go with the band name, but he was also the drummer. Plus, triple-X, get it?) Although it was only late afternoon, I was pretty sure that was Tommy Lee in the back corner pounding back shots. Hard to say, really, because he was half-covered by two groupies of his own.

"Shit," Keith Singerrr (the vocalist—big surprise) muttered. "Ono's here."

"Knock it off," Jefff said, punching him in the arm. Keith flipped him the bird, but shut up.

Keith was mad because I'd thrown him over for Jefff, who played bass. Let's face it (not that I'd tell my daughter this), I'd slept with them all at least once, once or twice with more than one at a time. But Jefff was my favorite, and you want to deal with big egos? Musicians' egos are bigger than their hair, and Angrrr Management was well on their way to single-handedly destroying the ozone layer.

I wish I'd thought of buying stock in Aqua Net.

Keith didn't have a leg to stand on, anyway. He was crashing at my place like the rest of them, passing out on the living room floor, the sofa, the other half of my narrow bed every night. I fed them ramen and hot dogs, kept them supplied with Jack and guitar strings, cleaned up their puke, made sure they got to gigs on time.

Hell, I bought their makeup.

"I thought you were at work," Jefff said, fondling my knee under the table. At least, I thought it was his hand.

"Yeah, small problem there. You know how I was handing out your demo tape? Against Tower Records' policies. They fired my ass."

Oh, yeah, I'd paid for their demo session, too.

I'd gone to the apartment, and Gina, who either lived next door or was the building's favorite hooker-on-call, told me the band said they were going to the Rainbow Room.

"No problem," Jefff said, his glossed smile wide. "We're hittin' the big time. We just got a manager!"

Weird as it sounds, until that moment I hadn't noticed the suit in the booth. Then, my eyes still wanted to slide over him rather than focus

131

on him.

My gut clenched. Something was very wrong.

"You signed already?"

"Mr. Nicholas had the gnarliest idea, too," Keith said. "We all got tattoos to celebrate."

Four forearms slapped down on the table to display four bright red tridents. Because the company, I swiftly learned, was called Pitchfork Promoters.

Angrrr Management were four talented guys. (They really were. I wasn't just some starry-eyed groupie; I knew decent music and I knew stage presence.) Talented, yes, and awfully pretty, all of them.

And every last one of them was dumber than a post.

Had they never heard of Robert Johnson?

Apparently not, because they'd gotten their tattoos at a parlor at the crossroads of Hollywood and Vine.

Van Halen's "Running With the Devil" was blaring through the club, and the band was whooping and toasting with shots and snorting lines (a celebratory present from Mr. Nicholas), and I closed my eyes and muttered, "Oh, hell."

I heard a low, otherworldly chuckle.

I went to Mr. Nicholas's office the next day, determined to do...something.

I wore the most suit-like professional outfit I had. Granted, it was pale pink and satiny, but the skirt came down below my knees (skinny, with a big slit up the back) and the blazer had some amazing shoulder pads that made me feel confident and strong.

Until I walked into his office, and he smiled a toothy smile and said with a body like mine, he could totally make me a star. Gag me with a spoon.

"I know who you are," I said. "Totally. So don't try to trick me." He probably would try, anyway. I hoped to hell I wouldn't mess up.

I asked if I could take a copy of the contract with me, but he said no. Damn. In the back of my trunk was a battered box of my first-year law books, including Contracts. I'd gotten through a whole year before I ditched the school and started driving west.

So I did my best to ignore him while I poured through the tiny print legalese. There were pages and pages of it. I swallowed, fighting back panic.

"What does this mean?" I asked, pointing at a clause. "How can you guarantee to get them a major record deal?"

"Oh, that." He leaned back, the leather of his chair creaking, and clasped his hands behind his head. Obviously confident enough in his abilities that it wasn't worth lying to me. "Simple, really. Their Friday night gig at the Roxy? At my invitation, there'll be several record execs in the audience. And I'll give the boys amazing talent, so the execs will have to bite."

In exchange, the contract's convoluted wording said, buried on page thirty-six, was each guy's soul.

"Is there anything I can do to convince you to break the deal?" I asked.

He sniffed. "You're hardly a virgin, but your soul's still sweet.

Which one's your favorite? I'll let you trade your soul for his."

I'd have been offended if the lack-of-virginity part wasn't true. At any rate, as fond as I was of Jefff, I wasn't going to abandon the whole group. "Not good enough."

That oily smile again. "You could take me up on my offer to make you a star. You'd be even more fun than them."

"No!"

He leaned forward, scowling. I don't care what they say about hell being hot—the room dropped twenty degrees, I swear.

"Miss Patrick, you are trying my patience," he said. "This is supposed to be fun, and you're making it not fun anymore. So you know what I'm going to do? Friday night, after they get their record deal? That's when I'm taking their souls. They're all going to die."

Not if I could help it.

Fact was, I had enough drugs and alcohol in my system to believe I could take on the Devil. In the back of my mind, I knew that if I failed, he'd find some way to take my soul, but I was too—let's call it "focused"—to care.

I had only a day to pull it off.

Friday night, Angrrr Management played an incredible gig. There were some equipment flub-ups, sure, but they sounded totally bitchen'. Afterwards, in the closet that passed as a dressing room, they were approached by not one, not two, but three major labels.

I made them promise they wouldn't sign anything without me, and went out to the dance floor.

"I hope you've had your chance to say goodbye," Mr. Nicholas said, looking dapper in a pin-striped suit and skinny tie. "I'm afraid they're all going to be in a tragic, drug-fueled car accident tonight. No survivors."

"I don't think so," I shouted above the next band (something about roses and guns) who'd just taken the stage. "Your contract's invalid."

"Impossible," he hissed.

"Totally, dude. They didn't get the record contract because you helped them."

"I gave them exceptional musical talent."

"But nobody heard it. They were lip-synching. I turned off their amps and fed their demo recordings through." I smiled. I had a right to be smug. "They got the record deal on their own talent."

His shriek of anger was lost in the wail of guitars.

Angrrr Management broke up before they recorded their first album. Some of the members went on to moderate success in other metal bands, although under different names.

As for me, I was lucky enough to escape the eighties without an STD, a drug problem, or another encounter with the Devil.

Well, sort of.

I went back to law school, got my degree. But I went into entertainment law, fighting on the side of the poor stupid artists who, without proper guidance, would sign just about anything to be famous.

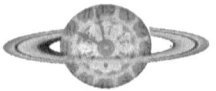

An interviewer once said of **Dayle A. Dermatis**, "she has so many aliases, you'd think she was a spy!" A dabbler in several genres (and with several coauthors), she's sold two novels to Virgin Books and short stories in multiple genres: romance, erotica, fantasy/SF, and media tie-in. Her fantasy stories appear in *The Trouble With Heroes* (DAW), *Fabulous Whitby* (Shrew Press, UK), and *The Pagan Anthology of Short Fiction: 13 Prize Winning Tales* (Llewellyn Publications, as Sophie Mouette), among others. She loves books, Styx, cats (big and small), Wales, TV, magic, laughter, and defying expectations. Her website is www.cyvarwydd.com.

Art Deco and the Infestation of New America

Paul Abbamondi

I t didn't take long.

The spreadheads left the hive in the morning, returned before our windows darkened. I awarded each one a treat: a second layer of skin, with a wide selection of opulent colors and textures. Most took the terra-cotta sunburst design, buzzing affectionately and twisting their antler-like antennae before turning in for the night to recharge. The extra skin served no purpose, purely decorative.

After I ate, I sent my servants away and sat window-side, waiting, darkness filling my belly. My beautiful system matrices dissolved and digested all the nasty slants no one wanted to claim, and I felt good, ready for the beauty of New America to unfold.

À bientôt.

In the morning, all was evident.

Buildings were grander, taller, affluent with a number of motifs, and ornamented streets arrowed their way through big cities and small towns alike with the ferocity of the hive's strongest spreadhead. Lucid colors eviscerated the bland. Women wore sharkskin dresses, men donned suits as shiny as wax apples, and everyone smiled, everyone danced.

Cameras flashed, spectacular big band songs played when cars honked, and the air glistened lime and violet. Status reports downloaded directly to me, and approval ratings were a solid *yes*. To counter this, I ate more filth.

The infestation had begun.

One pocket of the country resisted, a large area, and I drove the hive into a panic. Not because I had to—in time, the infestation would turn the pocket inside out, filling its walls with beauty and art and removing all forms of austerity, whether they be people, places, or things—but because I was cranky. Eating garbage hour-in, hour-out to make New America a better place took a toll on me. Motherhead had said it would, and I, being I, dismissed the warning.

After all, it was *I* that had spread the art in France, where it started, in Spain, and in the land of the *bouledogue*, so quirky.

Unnerved, I ate something horrible, washed it down with silt-brown water. Moments after, a servant updated me: every building along the East Coast had sprouted wings, as well as crystal-rimmed dimples that have caused many to stop and admire. They are calling it a miracle.

As they should.

Spreadheads are greedy things. I should know; I used to be one. After last week's panic attack, they went to work getting that New American pocket evolved. Some stung, some sprayed, some sacrificed themselves in ways that even I can't stomach. And then they came to me, one line of them, an entire hive's worth of buzzing and twitching, all of them demanding a reward.

And I gave it to them: a third layer of skin.

This layer was more eclectic, streamlined, and—something I did not initially account for—heavier. No longer just decorative.

The spreadheads wore the *avant-garde* skin proudly, filling the hive with buzz, but they flew slower and had a harder time reaching great heights. Training data showed sting speed dropping by a quarter. Worried, I requested the skin back. They refused. Then I demanded it, but they still refused. Motherhead ignored me, and more and more spreadheads moved out of their high-rise holes to live on the bottom floor.

De rien, greedy things.

New America is art, and art is love. There's even a banner of this stretched across the hive. Not my idea, but it's a nice reminder of what we've worked for. What we continue to work for. Alas, no one expected New Americans to get *bored*, especially so soon.

The trend went like this: building, chromatic building, building with wings, flying building...*oh, is that all?*

Motherhead ordered the hive to get to work, and the servants brought me more garbage. Barely even five barrels. The spreadheads were losing it. If we didn't keep New America entranced it would revert, revert hard, and everyone remembered what happened to New China when it went Old last summer. Motherhead would eat me, that much was certain.

I snailed over to the window to watch the spreadheads depart.

They dropped like rocks through the atmosphere, and data predicted most would die on impact. Too much skin. Not enough left in the hive to impress a few city-states. It was over. The infestation, the work, the pain in my stomach—all of it over.

My servants disappeared; I knew why.

The hive was already moving south to try elsewhere, regain our numbers. Ordered, spreadheads shed their second and third skins and burned them in the boiler room. Everyone was told to lay low, drink up, take care of their eggs.

Everyone but me.

Motherhead waited to summon me until my system matrices had finished cleaning out all the filth I ate to make New America what it was, when it was beautiful, when it was happy. Her cruelty was irrefutable: she wanted me at my best before being self-sacrificed. Some other spreadhead will take my spot, and I can't help but feel saddened over this. I was just trying to make the world crystalline, beautiful again, to give it color and angles and structures to admire. At the same time, I was trying to better the hive. It didn't work. It never will.

I chose to fly to Motherhead. The elevator seemed silly, and it'd been weeks since I'd been light enough to take flight; felt good, flying high and fiercely, catching hive-made updrafts and drifting further than I'd ever gone, but it had to end eventually. I landed outside her large bypass doors, taking in their symmetry, their indigo-and-azure glamour and brightness. They slid open soundlessly, perfunctorily, and I went to Motherhead much the same.

Adieu.

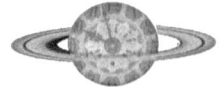

Paul Abbamondi reads and writes speculative fiction compulsively from somewhere in New Jersey. His short stories have appeared in *Shimmer*, *Farrago's Wainscot*, *Kaleidotrope*, as well as the two previous Raven Electrick Ink anthologies. He enjoys all things weird. Especially art-spreading bugs. In his spare time, he draws comics and wastes many late-night hours on videogames. You can send him e-mails at pdabbamondi@gmail.com. He likes e-mails.

The Darkness Whispers
(Flagstaff, AZ 1930)

Ann K. Schwader

Again tonight, the search for Planet X
goes on, though Lowell's gone these fourteen years,
& Mars Hill sure gets lonesome in the dead
of January. Tombaugh aims the 'scope
toward Gemini's black interstices, hoping
for two good plates in three, some hint of motion
beyond bleak Neptune lurking at the rim.

Beyond the rim of human comprehension,
the darkness whispers...& strange aether wakens
to speed the journeying of Those Outside.

Almost a month slips by before those plates
claim his attention. Sifting, shifting stars
& asteroids like sand grains in his eyes,
he stares into the blink comparator
until a single pinprick in the background
reveals/conceals/reveals its affirmation
of everything that Lowell died believing.

Of everything belief can teach of demons
when outer darkness whispers, so men's dreams
reveal the lineaments of Those Outside.

The news of Planet X—soon Pluto—breaks
on Lowell's birthday, though his mausoleum
sleeps mute as ever in the stubborn snows
of spring at altitude. Tombaugh delivers
the word himself—then lingers, puzzling
at footprints sunk bear-deep, but pincer-clawed
like some crustacean foreign to this earth.

Like some tongue foreign to our waking minds,
a darkness whispers: Yuggoth, new-found Yuggoth,
the outpost & the gate of Those Outside.

"—and I wish, for reasons I shall soon make clear, that the new
planet beyond Neptune had not been discovered."

~ H.P. Lovecraft, "The Whisperer In Darkness" (1930)

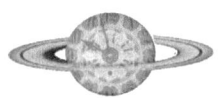

Ann K. Schwader's fifth speculative poetry collection, *Wild Hunt
of the Stars*, is due out from Sam's Dot Publishing in 2010. Her SF/dark

poetry has been published widely since the mid-1980s in such venues as *Mythic Delirium*, *Strange Horizons*, *Weird Tales*, *Space & Time*, and elsewhere. She is an active member of both HWA and SFWA, with multiple Honorable Mentions in *Year's Best Fantasy and Horror*. A Wyoming native, she now lives and writes in Colorado.

Mercury 13—And Beyond

Brenta Blevins

After the pioneer chimps first took Earthlings into space,

NASA recruited its astronaut corps:

the brave women of Mercury 13.

Rosie the Riveter

turned

Astrid the Astronaut.

From an engineering perspective,

it came down to simple physics:

females were the obvious choice;

their lighter bodies had smaller appetites

for food, air, and rocket fuel.

Although there were complaints from men

who demanded equal testing,

no-nonsense Vice-President Johnson scribbled it to a halt,

"Let's stop this. Now."

The first female President of the United States,

Jerrie Cobb, doesn't think her work in astronautics

solely launched her political vehicle,

but concedes it didn't hurt

to first punch through the ceiling of the sky

before piloting the country.

She jokes, "A woman was thrown out of court for

wearing slacks,

while the Mercury 13 women went to work in pantsuits—

silver, flashy, and not at all demure."

We all believed in her campaign slogan to dream higher;

billions of us had already thrilled at her tinny words

(still echoing in our minds)

as she descended the ladder of the Diana

and placed her boot in the powdery gray regolith of the

moon:

"That's one small step for a woman,

one giant leap for humankind."

With women forming the majority of NASA's ranks,

President Cobb says now that we've overcome the

obstacles,

she'd like to see more men working in astronautics

as NASA prepares for the first human mission to Mars in

1988.

To pique children's interest in space,

the president has written science fiction for young adults,

which she says her nieces love.

"I'd like for all humanity to keep leaping forward;

the sky is not the limit."

As for her own dream?

The President glances at a photo of her young nephew.

"That one day more boys—and girls—will read science

     fiction

and make it science fact."

Brenta Blevins lives and writes in the Appalachian Mountains, where she enjoys hiking with her husband. She has written audio dramas that have been produced for public radio in the United States and have aired there, in South Africa, and Australia. Her short fiction has appeared in *ChiZine*, *Sword and Sorceress*, and a number of anthologies, including *Sporty Spec: Games of the Fantastic*.

Nucleon

David D. Levine

"Tatyrczinski," he said, extending his hand. "Karel Tatyrczinski." His blue eyes sparkled under bushy white eyebrows, set in a round pink face. Wispy white hair tried, and failed, to cover a shiny pink scalp. That clean pink and white head emerged from the world's grimiest coverall. It was a fascinating contrast; I thought he'd make a great colored-pencil sketch. I liked him immediately.

I took the hand and shook it. "Pleased to meet you, Mr. Tat... um..."

"Tatter-zin-ski," he repeated. "Call me Carl. What are you looking for, Mr....?"

"James. Phil James. It's kind of difficult to explain. I'll know it when I see it."

"Well," he said, extending his hands to encompass the piles of objects all around him, "whatever it is, I've got it." I was inclined to believe him.

STUFF FOR SALE read the sign above the gate, matching the one-line listing in the Yellow Pages that had led me to this place. It was way, *way* off the beaten path; I was glad I'd called ahead for directions.

The name was apt. A stolid 1920's Craftsman-style house, with an unfortunate skin condition of yellow 1970's asphalt shingles, sat in the middle of piles and piles of...stuff. Heaps of sinks. Stacks of televisions.

Three barrels of shoes. File cabinets labeled CHAINS, DOORKNOBS, ALTERNATORS. A haphazard-looking structure of pipes and blue plastic sheeting kept the rain off the more fragile pieces, but a row of toilets standing by the fence wore beards of moss. The piles went on and on...he must have had at least a couple of acres. Through a window I saw that the house was just as crowded inside.

"I'm a commercial artist," I explained. "I'm doing a series of illustrations I call 'junklets'—gadgets made of junk. It's for a new ad campaign. The company wants to show how innovative and inventive it is. So what I need is stuff that *looks* interesting, things I can put together with other things in my pictures. It doesn't matter what it is, or whether or not it works." I pulled my digital camera out of my coat pocket. "Actually, all I need is reference photos. But I can pay you for your time."

"No need. I'm always glad to help an artist." He rubbed his chin with a grime-encrusted hand. The work-hardened skin scratched against his beard stubble. "Lessee. I think I had some old dentist equipment..." Suddenly he burst into motion and I had to scramble to keep up.

Down an alley of refrigerators, right turn at an old monitor-top Frigidaire, hard left at an ancient glass-fronted Coke machine, and there we were at a barrel of dental drills from the early 1900's. All joints and cables and black crinkle-finish metal struts, it looked like a family reunion of daddy longlegs. "This is great!" I said. I snapped a dozen pictures of the barrel just as it stood, then asked him to haul out a few choice pieces for closer examination. I wanted dozens of jointed arms for my Shoe-Tying Machine, and these would be perfect. "What else have you got that's like this? Mechanical. Early Twentieth Century stuff."

"Hmm. Follow me." And he was off again, past racks of doors and windows, with me trailing in his wake. A moment later he was lifting a blue tarp from a huge shelving unit, revealing ranks of radios: streamlined Bakelite Emersons, shiny chrome Bendixes, squat, blocky Motorolas. A harvest of design from the 20's to the 50's.

"These are phenomenal! I love old radios!"

"Most of 'em don't work any more, I'm afraid..."

"I don't care." I picked up a sleek Emerson from the 30's. The original ivory finish had yellowed, but it was in gorgeous shape. "They just don't design things like this any more. How much do you want for it?"

"Twenty-five. Naah, make it twenty-two fifty."

"I'll take it." I tucked the radio under my arm. "But. These are too...unitary. For my junklets I need parts. Moving parts."

"I know just the thing." He zipped through a gap between two piles of tires. Juggling the radio and my camera, I followed as best I could.

The entire afternoon went like that. I filled the camera's memory—over three hundred images—and wound up taking home two boxes of stuff as well. Not that I needed any of it, not that I had room for any of it, but it was all just fabulous. How could I leave this keen little eggbeater behind? I'd never seen another one like it. I put most of my finds on my knickknack shelves as soon as I got home.

After dinner I transferred the pictures into my computer, then started sorting, organizing, and cogitating. The hydraulic cylinder from the old forklift could support the seat of that office chair, and I could pull in the control panel from the red generator as well. By the time I reluctantly shut down at 3 AM I had images for a dozen junklets sorted into folders.

Bright and early the next day—by which I mean noon—I booted up my computer again and put a big newsprint pad on my drawing board. All afternoon I sketched, popping up images on the monitor whenever I needed reference or inspiration. Most of my friends think I'm weird, using paper and pencil to draw images from a computer screen, but it works for me. I've never been comfortable drawing with a mouse or a stylus, but managing reference photos with a computer beats shuffling piles of prints.

Three days later I was back at STUFF FOR SALE again. "Carl, the pictures I got last time were great. I need some more. What have you got that's big and flat and heavy and goes around?"

"What, like an old record player?"

"Yeah, but bigger."

"I think I might have something for you." He took me to a huge rotating platform, must have weighed a ton, made of rusty waffle-patterned iron. Neither of us could figure out what it had originally been used for, but it would be a perfect base for my Plastering Machine. While we were clearing some mannequins out of the way so I could get far enough back for a good photo, the bell on the front gate rang. "'Scuse me while I tend to a paying customer," Carl said.

"Take your time," I replied. "I can look around on my own." Carl vanished down a row of bookcases.

After I finished up with the platform, I wandered around. I

needed a big, tubby body for the Automated Barber, some tubes and pipes for the Plant Waterer, and a whole lot of irons for the Ironing Machine. But everywhere I went, all I found was...junk. Boxy, boring washing machines. Cracked water bottles. Hundreds of olive-drab ammo cases. Rusty metal shelving. I took a picture of a row of vending machines because I thought it was a nice composition, but I didn't see anything remotely useful for my project. I was getting pretty frustrated when Carl returned.

"I haven't found anything. Where's the good stuff?"

"It's all good stuff, to the right person. What are you looking for?"

"Well, first off, something with a round, tubby body. Person-sized."

"I know just the thing." He jogged down the row of washing machines, took a left turn. "How's this?" he asked, gesturing to a bulbous chrome 1950's water cooler.

"It's perfect!" I started snapping pictures, but something nagged at me. "Wait a minute. I was just here a minute ago. I stood on this very spot and took a picture of those vending machines over there. See?" I paged back through my stored pictures, showed him the vending machines on the camera's screen. "This water cooler is just what I was looking for. Why didn't I see it before?"

"I dunno. It hasn't moved lately." Indeed, there was grass growing through the holes in its base. How could I have missed it? "Sometimes folks can't find what they're looking for even if it's right in front of them. Sometimes they need a little help. Speaking of which, can I help you find anything else?"

"Uh, yeah. Some irons. Clothes irons."

"Right over here." But as I followed, I couldn't help but look back over my shoulder at the water cooler. I would have sworn there was nothing interesting in this whole area.

I visited STUFF FOR SALE two more times in the next three weeks. Carl never failed to find just the gizmo, gewgaw, or whatchamacallit I needed to complete my drawings, and I never failed to buy something. I spent over two hundred dollars on old radios alone. But it was worth it. I had all the reference images I needed; I had inspiration; I was happy. I turned out more and better work in less time than I ever had since art school.

That was just the beginning. The agency loved my junklets. The client loved my junklets. The industry loved my junklets; I even got my name in *Advertising Age*. The client ordered a second series of junklets, then another. They used my Automated Barber as the background image on their corporate stationery.

With all that publicity, I was inundated with new clients. I soon found myself with more work than I could handle and more money than I'd ever imagined. But I knew I was just the flavor of the month; I'd seen other artists rise meteorically and then vanish just as quickly. So I got myself a financial adviser, kept my frugal lifestyle (well, mostly), and put the extra cash into mutual funds.

Everyone wanted junklets, or something like junklets. I was constantly in need of more mechanical images, more inspirations. I sometimes visited Carl three times in a week. We got to be pals.

One day we were sitting in Carl's kitchen, sharing a beer after a long hot afternoon tramping around the junkyard. "Tell me, Phil," he said, "how did you get into this crazy advertising business anyway?"

I thought about it for a moment. "I suppose you'd have to blame my dad. He was an automotive designer at Ford. When I was a kid I'd visit him at his office during the summer; he'd always let me play with his colored pencils. I guess that's where I caught the art bug."

"Ford, eh? Did your dad design anything I might have seen?"

"He was on the team that did the '66 Fairlane. But mostly he did conceptual designs. It was exciting for him to be out beyond the cutting edge like that, but he was always disappointed that none of his designs made it into actual production." I took a swig of my beer. "He worked on the Nucleon."

Carl put down his beer. "Nucleon?"

"It was a concept car for a World's Fair or something like that. A nuclear-powered car, can you believe it? Atoms for peace."

Carl got a strange look on his face then. "I have something out back that I think you ought to see."

The sun was low in the sky, casting neon-orange glints off the hoods of a row of old cars all the way at the back of the yard, where we'd seldom gone before. Bees buzzed in the shrubs that grew along the fence. Near one end of the row was a bulky shape shrouded in a moss-covered, olive-drab tarp. "Help me haul this off, would you?"

We pulled off the tarp and revealed one of the strangest-looking cars you've ever seen. It looked like a cross between an old Caddy with big pointed fins and a pickup truck, and where the trunk, or pickup bed, should have been there was a big square hole that went all the way down to the ground. It looked like a car with a built-in swimming pool.

It was painted in that Godawful turquoise color that was so popular in the Fifties.

On the tailgate was a name in chrome script: Nucleon.

"Sonofabitch! You've got the mockup! I didn't even know they built one!"

"Take a closer look."

I looked. It was no fiberglass mockup. It was real steel, and a little rusty. The doors were scarred with parking-lot dings. The tires were bald. The seats and the steering wheel were worn from use. The odometer showed seventy-one thousand and some miles.

There was no gas gauge.

Suddenly I got a queasy feeling in the pit of my stomach. "Carl... do you, by any chance, have...a Geiger counter?"

"You know, I think I might. Hang on a sec."

I just stood and stared slack-jawed at the thing while Carl left and came back.

"Here it is."

"Check out the back first. The reactor was really heavy; it had its own wheels. It rode in that hole, kind of like a trailer only surrounded by the car." Carl waved the Geiger counter's wand around inside the hole. There was a slight increase in the chattering noise it made, but only a little. "Any idea how much radiation is too much?"

"Not a clue."

"Still, it doesn't seem too bad."

"No."

"But it's not zero. That means this car once had a nuclear reactor. It was a fucking *nuclear car!*"

"Jesus."

We sat in the grass, leaning our backs against a nearby Camaro, and watched the air shimmer over the Nucleon's sun-warmed roof. Crickets chirped. Carl plucked a long stalk of grass and chewed on it thoughtfully.

"Where did you get this thing, anyway?" I asked.

He stared off at the setting sun for a while, then shook his head. "Sorry, I don't remember. I know it wasn't here when I bought the place back in '48."

"How can you forget buying an atomic car? You remember everything else about this place."

"It's a funny thing." He looked down into his cupped hands. "Usually it's pretty simple. Like, suppose you wanted a carburetor for a '52 Mercury. I'd know where to look, and I might find one or I might not. But sometimes, like with the Nucleon here"—he gestured at it with the stalk—"I remember exactly where it is, but I don't remember remembering it before, if you catch the distinction." He looked right at me then, his eyes hard. "I'm only telling you this because you're an artist. If I told my buddies at the VFW they'd have me locked up."

"My lips are sealed."

"I knew you'd understand."

The sun was setting behind the Nucleon, and the breeze was cooling. "What are we going to do with this thing?" I asked. "I sure don't have any place to park it."

"Cover it over with the tarp again, I guess. Maybe it'll be here tomorrow, maybe not. There's no telling."

We hauled the tarp back over that impossible car and walked back to the gate in silence. Then I turned to him and said, simply, "Thank you."

"You're welcome," he replied. He closed the gate behind me, and as I drove off I saw him sitting on the porch, staring off into the darkening sky.

After another year or so the blush was off the apple and I was no longer the hot new thing. Just as well, really; I was tired of junklets, tired of juggling assignments, tired of airports. I settled back into a career that was a lot like it had been before, only now I had a cushion of investments that meant I didn't have to hustle so hard between assignments. I was happy enough, I suppose, though sometimes I missed those crazy junklet days.

I was doing a lot of stuff based on natural forms and landscapes then, getting my reference photos on nature hikes, and I didn't see Carl very often. We always exchanged Christmas cards, though. Then one day I got a phone message from him: would I please come out to the yard, as soon as possible?

"Glad you could make it," he said as I walked up his porch steps the next day. He was sitting on a battered wire milk crate, looking like a broken gray umbrella. His health had been poor for months, though he rarely complained.

"No problem," I said. "How did you get my number?" He'd

never called before.

"It was on your checks. Listen, I know this is going to seem strange, but I found this at the bottom of a coffee can full of bolts and somehow I just knew it belongs to you." He held out a small metallic object.

It was a key, a scarred brass thing, one of those ones that's the same on both sides. Smaller than a car key, bigger than a suitcase key. "I don't recognize it."

"You're sure? I don't get these feelings often, and when I do they're usually right."

"I'm pretty sure. Sorry."

"Well, keep it anyway. Memento of an old man's folly. Sorry I dragged you out here for nothing."

"That's OK, I was thinking of coming out for a visit anyway." We spent a pleasant hour on the porch, watching the leaves fall and talking about contact lenses, fast food, and the weather. Then I bought some flowerpots and went home.

Two weeks later I got a call from Laurel Hernandez, Carl's lawyer. Carl had died in his sleep, at the age of 78, and I was mentioned in his will. The funeral was Tuesday; the will would be read the next week.

I met dozens of people at the funeral, all of whom Carl had touched in some significant way. A woman for whom Carl had found a vibrating chair that was the only thing that made her bad back tolerable. A man who had kept a fleet of delivery trucks going with spare parts from Carl's yard. A family that had rebuilt a shoddy old house into a showplace, using materials and fixtures provided by Carl, and helped to revitalize their whole neighborhood. We spent the afternoon swapping Carl stories; it was a sad occasion, but not somber.

The will reading was a lot less crowded. There was me, and Ms. Hernandez, and a clerk, and a couple of cousins. The cousins got the investments, which were not trivial. I got the junkyard.

I told Ms. Hernandez I needed a couple of days to think about my options. But I was only halfway down the stairs from her office when I realized I already knew exactly what to do. I sat down right there on the steps and cried, overwhelmed by the generosity of Carl's final gift.

Ms. Hernandez drove me out to the yard after the transfer of title, a complicated ceremony involving the signing of more papers than I'd ever seen in my life. "Are you sure you don't want me to find a management company to run the business for you?" she asked as we got out of the car.

"I'm sure. I plan to keep on as a contract artist part-time, at least for a while, but this is what I want to do. Where I want to be. However, I'd appreciate the services of an experienced business lawyer."

"I would be happy to help."

The gate was padlocked. I'd never seen it padlocked before.

I stood there for a moment, not knowing what to do, and then I put my hands in my jacket pockets and felt something hard. It was the key Carl had given me the last time I saw him, which was also the last time I'd worn that jacket.

On impulse, I tried it in the padlock.

It worked.

We got inside and wandered around the yard. Ms. Hernandez didn't seem to think it was odd that I had a key to the gate, and I decided not to mention the circumstances under which I'd acquired it.

We paused before a rank of vacuum cleaners, a faded rainbow of aqua and pink and beige plastic. "Mr. Tatyrczinski was one of my favorite clients," Ms. Hernandez said. "He gave me a bust of Kennedy for my birthday one year. Kennedy was my hero, but I don't think I ever mentioned that to him. Somehow he always knew just the right thing to do."

"Maybe he didn't know. Maybe the junkyard knew."

"What?"

"Never mind. Wait a minute, I just remembered something." I walked down to the end of the row of appliances, paused a moment, turned left. There, on a battered chrome dinette table, was a jar of buttons. I opened it, dug around for a moment. "Here. I think Carl would have liked you to have this."

It was a campaign pin in red, white, and blue. It was a little faded, but still plainly readable: RE-ELECT JFK IN '64.

"This must have been some kind of joke," Ms. Hernandez said.

"Maybe. Or maybe it's a little memento from a time that never was. A time that was better than this one."

"What a...a lovely thought. In any case, if I were your business lawyer I would caution you against giving away merchandise to friends and relatives. It's a common problem for new business owners."

"OK, I'll take three bucks for it. Naah, make it two fifty."

"It's a deal."

We stood side by side and watched the sun set over the junkyard.

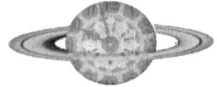

David D. Levine is a writer of science fiction and fantasy short stories whose work has appeared in *Fantasy & Science Fiction*, *Asimov's*, *Realms of Fantasy*, *Analog*, and anthologies including four Year's Best volumes. His stories have won several awards, including the Hugo, and have been nominated for many others. A collection of his short stories, *Space Magic*, is available from Wheatland Press. He lives in Portland, Oregon, with his wife Kate Yule, with whom he publishes the fanzine *Bento*.

"Nucleon" first appeared in *Interzone*, December 2001.

About the Editor

Karen A. Romanko has seen over 100 of her poems and short stories published in venues such as *Strange Horizons*, *Aberrant Dreams*, *Ideomancer*, and *The Pedestal Magazine*. She is editor of two speculative fiction and poetry anthologies, *Sporty Spec: Games of the Fantastic* (2007) and *Cinema Spec: Tales of Hollywood and Fantasy* (2009), both from Raven Electrick Ink.

When not hunched at the computer, she enjoys the sun of Southern California with her biologist husband, Bob Desharnais. A long-time movie buff, Karen loves the proximity to Tinseltown, but misses the fall foliage of her native Boston and always roots for the Red Sox.

www.ingramcontent.com/pod-product-compliance
Lightning Source LLC
Chambersburg PA
CBHW050751250626
47155CB00005B/2022